A Battle More Desperate

"Greater love hath no man than this,

that a man lay down his life for his friends."

John 15:13

Randy Pilz

ISBN 978-0-9971114-1-5 (paperback)

Cover Design by Valerie Pilz

All Bible quotations taken from the King James Version

Any images, maps and illustrations used are taken from those in the Public Domain or adapted from them. Cover photo of G.I.'s on the snowy road is "Bulge_stvithroad_1945jan24_375" from the National Archives. "Wacht Am Rhein Map" is from the US ARMY Center for Military History.

Boeletus Media – Attalla, Alabama 2015

DEDICATION

Remembering my father, Richard Pilz, Sr., an Army Air Forces veteran of

World War II, with affection and gratitude for instilling in me a love for

reading, an abiding interest in my country's history and an admiration and

respect for her men and women in uniform past and present.

ACKNOWLEDGMENTS

I thank the Lord for planting the story idea and guiding in its development. This work began years ago as a drama, *The Greatest Love*, performed as part of the 1994 Christmas program at Falls Baptist Church in Menomonee Falls, WI in commemoration of the 50th Anniversary of the Battle of the Bulge. I'm grateful also for the support and encouragement of the church family at Falls Baptist back then and for the trust and encouragement of the pastoral and music staffs at that time, especially Senior Pastor Wayne Van Gelderen, Jr. and Associate Pastor Brad Blanton. The seed planted long ago has borne further fruit in the form of this novel.

It was one thing to write a play and another, longer creative journey to transform and expand that same story into a novel. I thank the Lord also for the love and patience of my wife and children over the years as I struggled in learning the novelist's craft. They wondered if any novelization would ever see the light of day. By God's grace, that dawn has come at long last.

Map showing the "bulge" created by westward advancing German forces during *Wacht Am Rhein* ("Watch on the Rhine"), their code-name for the counter-offensive, better known to Americans as "The Battle of the Bulge."

INTRODUCTION

As the campaigns of World War II raged around the globe, unsung heroes waged another desperate battle. Though their victories never made the headlines, their efforts wrought eternal results. As born-again believers in the armed forces, soldiers of the King of Kings and soldiers of their country, these men and women in uniform carried out the Great Commission, even while defeating the Axis, bearing the light of the gospel wherever they served.

PROLOGUE

Burnanski's Dream

Distant thunder.

Morning or afternoon? No way to tell. Dim light, diffused through an overcast sky, yields no clues in a fog-shrouded pine forest.

The forest is unfamiliar. You think, *Where is this?* Not like cultivated woodlands of England or ancient hedgerows of Normandy, not the low fields of Holland. Ravines and gullies cut across the uneven forest floor. A thick mat of needles spreads beneath the pines, wild and tangled undergrowth in places, patches of snow upon the open ground.

More thunder, louder, rolling nearer; but not thunder—more dangerous, destructive, deadly. Rolling closer, closer, closer, shaking the ground. You abruptly turn, break into a run, weaving through the trees.

Someone else is there! Turn to the right, weapon up, safety off, ready to fire. Another G.I., another trooper runs beside you. Too dim to see his face. Only his eyes gleam from the shadow beneath his helmet. *Who is this?*

KARAAK-BOOM! KARAAK-BOOM! A double flash, like complementary bolts of lighting, twin explosions shred the tops of nearby trees. White-hot metal scythes through the upper forest, sounding like sand sprayed through the higher limbs.

Fear drives you on, your heart pounding. Stumble, fall, the mystery soldier reaches down and pulls you up. You run again, behind him now, pace for pace.

Branches, chunks of wood, bark, and other debris raining to the ground. One slim defense against tree bursts when caught in the open within a forest: Shield yourself behind a great tree. You shout to the other soldier, "Grab a tree! Hug it! Keep your head down and hold on for dear life!"

Press your face against cold, rough bark. Squatting in the cold and waiting, enduring. Acrid smoke hangs like fog, mixed with the bitter odor of burnt pine. Eyes water. Hold a handkerchief over mouth and nose, still sputtering and coughing.

KARAAK-BOOM! KARAAK-BOOM! KARAAK-BOOM! The explosions come again, seeking you out. Hug the tree tighter; hope the barrage stops.

The silent soldier's a short distance away. *Who is he? What does he feel? Is he just as afraid?* Call to him, "Hey!"

His head turns toward you; he looks into your eyes. A young face, but unfamiliar. "Who *are* you?" you shout above the din.

KARAAK-BOOM! A flash. He's gone!

You're violently slammed against your own tree. The sound of the explosion rings in your ears and reverberates within your chest. Dirt and bits of wood splatter you. Blasted earth and a smoldering, shattered trunk where the other soldier crouched only a moment before. "No! No! No! Not again!"

Suddenly awake, bathed in a cold sweat, shaking from the nightmare. Still in the stockade, still under guard. Lie awake, trying to calm down, wondering about the dream. Rapid breathing and pulse subside. *Who was that soldier?*

Dawn comes slowly.

CHAPTER ONE

A U.S. Army Camp in Northern France

Early December 1944

Wilcox

Why did I let them talk me into this? Sergeant Anthony Wilcox chided himself for the hundredth time. He leaned against an interior wall beside a cracked casement window, trying to ease his painful back and focus on writing in his notebook journal. Between glances out of the rain-splattered glass and attacks of self-doubt, his notations came slowly. The view didn't distract as much as the doubt. Beyond the casement, regular clusters of gray buildings lined a long gravel road. Pockmarks blemished their stuccoed walls. The road's surface chewed up by the passage of heavy armored vehicles. Its ruts and potholes, recent battle scars, overflowed with rainwater. Machine gun and small arms fire accounted for damage on the buildings. Some structures were destroyed. Roofs gaped open. Boards covered many windows in others.

Wilcox pressed his back flat against the rough surface of the wall, trying to relax tightened muscles, easing his lower spine. He'd wrenched it, landing awkwardly in a beet field during the drop into Holland, about three months before. Living outdoors, sleeping in damp foxholes, and the wear and tear of combat hampered improvement. His lumbar muscles tightened-up following activity out in the cold, rainy weather earlier that morning, giving him grief again.

He needed rest, needed it badly. Not merely physical rest through decent nights of uninterrupted sleep, he needed a cleansing of the mind, the psyche, the soul. Combat fatigue some would call it. The horrors of war mark a man, never leave him unaffected. Each incident, each death wounds within. Ultimately, a man needed rest, an inner purging, otherwise he might lose control, breaking down mentally or breaking out in rage.

His squad was new, less than two days old, formed from remnants reshuffled within the battalion's units, spreading the veterans throughout the companies, moving some up into leadership. No one in his group served in the platoon's original 2nd Squad, as it was a year ago. Those men would never return. Headquarters promoted one of them out, while still recovering from his wounds. Two lay in hospitals over in England. Another was already on board a ship headed back to the states and artificial limbs. The rest had fallen in battle, in Normandy and especially in the Netherlands —an operation dragging on over 70 days of combat, much costlier than D-Day. Brother squads and platoons suffered losses as well. The entire company whittled down to the size of a reinforced platoon.

Maybe it's a mistake, Wilcox thought again. *I shouldn't have let them make me a squad leader, taken this on. Maybe I should quit, go on sick call, throw in the towel.*

Few in civilian life could appreciate how soul-weary soldiers steel themselves in times like this. Wilcox bent his mind to the task. *You're a historian,* he told himself. *Over a hundred and sixty years ago, the men of the Continental Army had their own desperate struggle, persevered and ultimately triumphed. You're of the same character, the same heritage.* However, those thoughts came up short in bolstering his spirit as his meditation continued, *But we're immersed in a horrendous form of warfare no one in Washington's army ever dreamed of in his worst nightmares.*

Beside the window, wrestling to win the battle within, Wilcox forced himself to stand still. Only the lid of his left eye twitched. Somehow, he had to deal with the tension coiled inside, for the good of himself and the squad.

His eye twitched again as he glanced out the cracked windowpane at the dreary morning, out toward the rutted road and the other dismal barracks. His gaze swept from left to right and back again, from horizon to foreground. It seemed one of them was always watching. The veterans, the survivors, had learned the stark necessity of careful vigilance in a violent school of life and death. One or more of them always looking out. Even now, many miles behind the lines, the cautious surveillance continued, slow to subside.

High command withdrew the division's remnants from combat less than a week before. Trucks brought them down to this ancient French Army base. The survivors now faced the daunting task of recovery, within themselves and as a fighting unit. Like Wilcox, battle had taken a toll on the men in his squad physically, mentally and emotionally to varying degrees (and on the larger formations to which they belonged—platoon, company, battalion, etc.). Their equipment situation a mess. Much of their gear needed repair or replacement.

Most of the squad members had minor wounds still healing. Wilcox examined the small scars on the backs of his hands and along his forearms, where mortar fragments had peppered him. He inspected the discolored middle finger of his left hand, missing a nail. *Hope it grows back,* he thought.

He turned to the window and wiped away condensation. He caught a vague glimpse of himself reflected back from the inside of the glass. Average in height and frame, with dark wavy hair. Twenty-five years old, but he appeared over ten years older now. His aching back made him feel even older than he looked. His eye twitched again. He shook his head at his reflection, *You're already an old man. If Mom could see me now!*

He heard the sounds of the squad in the narrow room behind him. Six double bunks crammed together in two rows. Parents back at the boarding school where he'd been a teacher would've complained if similar space in the dormitory held two beds. The retreating Wehrmacht had destroyed most furniture left by the surrendering French Army years before. American engineers supervised P.O.W.'s in slapping together simple bunks—rough-cut four-by-fours for the bedposts, two-by-fours for the frames. A musty, straw-filled mattress cover topped off a row of narrow wooden slats on each bed. *At least we're indoors and dry,* Wilcox thought, both a luxury compared the cold, muddy foxholes they'd inhabited less than two weeks ago.

At the rear center of the room sat a small, coal-burning stove salvaged from a bombed-out village somewhere, their meager source of heat. They'd strung paracord lines overhead near the stove. Outer garments, dampened during the morning run, hung on the lines, adding to the room's many odors. Most of his men sat on their bunks facing the stove, busy cleaning boots and other gear or just loafing around, waiting now for the call to mid-day chow.

At least I have a nucleus of veterans to build from, Wilcox thought. Of his men, Friedenfeld and Vincenti had combat experience in the recent Netherlands operation. Cooper had more experience, coming in with reinforcements on D+5, while the division still fought through the Norman hedgerows. Only Burnanski remained as seasoned an old-timer as Wilcox— the ever-decreasing ranks of those who'd first mustered with the unit during its earliest days on the red clay of Northeastern Georgia.

Corporal Henry Cooper, also newly promoted, served as assistant squad leader. An easy-going Brooklyn native, a bit taller and heavier than Wilcox. Cooper's lantern jaws sported a perpetually bluish beard shadow, and a toothpick of some kind habitually dangled from his mouth. That toothpick plus his dark beard-line gave him a gaunt, mobsterish appearance. He suffered wounds after the second week of fighting in Holland. Barely recovered, Cooper arrived ahead of the platoon at this camp. The most rested, mentally and physically of the squad. Wilcox requested Cooper in the deal he made with both the company captain and the major commanding their battalion when he agreed to become squad leader. He needed Cooper's buoyant personality to balance his quieter, cerebral disposition.

Privates Vincenti and Friedenfeld made another pair of balanced personalities. Vincenti, swarthy and streetwise, came from a first-generation Italian-American family in Philadelphia. No-nonsense Friedenfeld, a brown-haired German-American, hailed from a ranch outside Glendo, Wyoming.

Burnanski remained the odd man out. Tallest and most muscular of the group, dark and foreboding with deep-set eyes and high cheekbones. No one in the squad anywhere near capable of counterbalancing him. No one dared try. Busted back to private, *private* also the world into which he withdrew.

Wilcox glanced back from the window to where Burnanski lay on the top of a set of bunks, away from the door and farthest from the others. The big man stared up at the cracked ceiling, smoking his way through another pack of cigarettes. Scars hardly enhanced his rough features. Knuckles on his large hands also bore scars, his muscular forearms bruised and bandaged. His most recent wounds excused him from running out in the rain with the others, but were not combat-related—that is, not the result of combat with German forces.

Early that morning, M.P.'s brought Burnanski in. Visibly relieved, they signed him over to Wilcox and removed shackles. Wilcox knew Burnanski by association and reputation ever since they'd trained in brother units back in the states. After arriving, Burnanski immediately pulled himself up on the farthest bunk, lying there ever since. A personal request by the Captain and the Major, Wilcox must handle this hot potato—another part of the deal he'd made when he became squad leader, the toughest part: *Take Burnanski.*

Wilcox focused on his journal again. A lover of history and a teacher of it at a private academy in rural Pennsylvania, he'd read old diaries, first-hand accounts and journals from Revolutionary and Civil War veterans. Their writings inspired his. For now, the intended readers were his parents back in Pennsylvania. If he could somehow explain his war experiences and observations to them, perhaps others would understand as well. Knowing his mom and dad might read it kept him from using more colorful language that seasoned his vocabulary since entering the army.

He paused, trying to sum up the past few days of activity and put his pencil to paper again. His notations stopped in mid-sentence when his peripheral vision detected movement on the road outside. A jeep approached. He recognized the passenger, the Lieutenant, his new platoon's leader. Wilcox warned the others. "Stand by. The Lieutenant's coming."

Might not be good, Wilcox thought, *but inevitable.* His spirit groaned at being goaded back into activity again and groaned at having to goad others, also an inevitability. After all, the war raged on. "Time was of the essence," patriotic propagandists proclaimed, and airborne units prided themselves in accomplishing tasks "double time," and "on the hustle."

The jeep swerved around a large pothole. The driver, a skinny corporal from battalion headquarters. The young non-com handled the jeep with consummate skill gained from driving equipment on a Missouri farm since he was ten. The driver took his foot off the gas pedal and jerked the hand brake. The drab little vehicle slid to a halt through wet gravel in front of the barracks. Filthy water dripped from the jeep's tires, sides, and underbody. Wisps of steam wafted from its water-splattered exhaust pipe.

Within the barracks room, Cooper moaned. "Man! I just cleaned these boots! Hope the Lieutenant ain't takin' us out again!"

"No," Wilcox answered. He peered out of one of the uncracked windowpanes. "Changed uniforms. Got a tie on. Looks like something official."

"Mess call's soon," said Friedenfeld. "Hope he doesn't make us late."

"What's the trouble now?" Vincenti asked. He flicked the stiletto he'd been fiddling with, a prized memento from his days on the Philly streets. *Thunk!* It stuck into a nearby bedpost.

"If it's only a little trouble, I think he'd send Reynolds," reasoned Friedenfeld. "If it's big trouble he'll come himself. Must be big." He shot a cautious glance toward where Burnanski lay. Wilcox fought his own urge to look in Burnanski's direction. An awkward moment. Others silently fought the same urge, the automatic assumption that any trouble involving the squad involved Burnanski.

"Why do we think it's trouble at all?" asked Cooper, deflecting unspoken conclusions centering on "the elephant in the room." He suggested a cheerful spin, "Maybe it'll be good. Maybe our turn for Paris."

"Not likely," Vincenti sneered.

Wilcox agreed. Misery had become so familiar that he could see it coming with his eyes closed. "The Captain or the Major will call us out for that," he said. "Give a little personal pep talk and a fatherly warning. The Lieutenant's coming out to us. Something else is up." He knew enough of company operations to figure that much out. Until now, except for cursory inspections, officers had stayed out of the barracks. Reynolds, the company's senior NCO, was the main sanctum intruder the past couple of days.

Everyone loathed activity in general. Lethargy and apathy had set in, replacing the constant stress of the combat zone. Now the Lieutenant might prod them into some field problem or additional physical training. Reluctant to get moving, the men must stay in shape and keep their skills sharp. Battlefield survival depended on it. *Have to get them up and push them along*, Wilcox thought. *Push myself to push them.* His left eyelid twitched in response to the idea.

Wilcox watched the Lieutenant wait for a truck and trailer to splash by before getting out of the jeep. He took pains to preserve his fresh uniform. Wilcox had seen this situation develop before, immediately after returning from Normandy. It still miffed him how the officers became picky about uniforms and regulations so quickly again. Just shy of 26 years old, the tall, muscular Lieutenant possessed a broad face, a jutting chin, and a nose flattened while playing guard on the varsity football team at The Citadel, South Carolina's state military college. His barracks cap covered a head of thinning sandy-colored hair.

Wilcox watched the Lieutenant avoid yet another mud puddle as he crossed the road. Everywhere there seemed to be mud. A familiar thought crossed Wilcox's mind: *Perhaps the ancient etymology of the name Europe was "Land of Mud."* The troopers encountered a lot of it the past six months. Sometimes, the mud was thin and soupy, like the pothole puddles along the road right now. More often, the mud they struggled with was thick and gelatinous. Gray, black, reddish brown--the deeper stuff could suck the boots off the feet of any G.I. slogging through it. As airborne assault troops fighting on the front lines, they had lived in it, slept in it, fought in it, would likely die in it.

Beyond the Lieutenant, Wilcox could see a distant portion of the large parade ground. Now that the rain had stopped, companies from a brother battalion suffered through close-order drill. They marched and counter-marched in precise rhythm to call and response cadence chants led by their company's sergeants. The drill itself won't help any of them in battle. None of Wilcox's units had yet to march, row after row, through the flower-throwing, grateful population of some newly liberated city. Folks back home saw those scenes on newsreels and assumed they were common place. Not that the division hadn't been liberators of towns and villages, but most of their liberating occurred under heavy fire as troopers darted from doorway to doorway down rubble-strewn, smoke-clouded streets. Too busy killing the enemy and trying to keep from being killed to parade through town before pushing on to the next objective. Close-order drill had a place right now only for keeping powers of concentration sharp, fostering military discipline, teamwork and *esprit de corps*.

The Lieutenant strode up the gravel path to Wilcox's building.

"Almost to the door," Wilcox reported to the others in the room.

"Bar the door!" sneered Vincenti. His stiletto flashed across the room. Thunk! It stuck into a bedpost below Burnanski. Vincenti grimaced over at Wilcox and shrugged, his eyes saying, *"I forgot."*

Without expression or even glancing over at the stiletto, one of Burnanski's large hands reached down and closed over the handle. A quick flick of his wrist as he snapped the knife. The tip of the blade remained embedded in the wood. The broken hasp and handle clattered to the floor. Burnanski flicked ash from his cigarette and continued staring.

"My best knife," Vincenti muttered.

Wilcox shot a stern look back at Vincenti—the scolding frown reserved for malefactors in his classrooms—an unspoken message: *"I warned you: Steer clear of Burnanski!"*

Cooper stepped over and kicked the knife handle clattering back across the floor to Vincenti. "Momma says, 'if you don't play nice, your toys will be taken away!'"

Wilcox returned his gaze out the window and saw the Lieutenant had paused before their dwelling's entrance, fists on hips. Their lucky platoon sheltered in an actual building rather than large, drafty army-issued pyramidal tents like some units. (The regimental commander insisted that line troops most exposed to the elements in recent combat receive priority in whatever indoor billets available for enlisted men.) This particular stucco building divided into four rooms side by side. Each room barely large enough for a squad of 12 men. The entire structure housed roughly an airborne platoon all together. Three similar barracks buildings (the remainder of the company's enlisted men) shared latrines and showers (bucolic French versions thereof), located in a semi-enclosed structure next door.

A rifle grenade blew out the doorway to Wilcox's new domicile when U.S. infantry flushed Wehrmacht units out of the area at the end of the summer. Work crews fabricated a replacement door and door frame out of plywood and scrap lumber salvaged from packing crates. What made the Lieutenant pause wasn't the entry itself but the squad's makeshift Christmas decorations adorning it. No specific order forbade them from festooning the doorway. Inspired by the free-spirited Cooper, they spent part of the previous Sunday afternoon "decking the halls," or rather, the entrance thereof, with makeshift décor, competing with the rest of the company. Other squads in the platoon conspired in the creative project, keeping watch and scrounging materiel. A scraggly arch of pine boughs framed the top of the entry, hiding most of the blackened stucco above the door. A large wreath (fabricated by Vincenti and Friedenfeld), accented with empty grenade casings in place of pine cones (Cooper's idea) and a red bow, fashioned out of strips of fabric cut from a worn air-recognition panel (Wilcox's contribution), hung on the unpainted plywood door itself. Less than two weeks ago, dug in on a dike near the Neder Rijn, they lived a day-to-day, hour-to-hour, and often minute-to-minute existence. Now, away from the front and with Christmas approaching, they looked forward to something with enjoyment instead of dread.

There seemed to be good reason for their optimism. Back in June, the Allies landed in Normandy. Through the summer into early autumn, they roared across most of France and into Belgium, driving the Wehrmacht back toward the Rhine. Many, from lofty generals down to the dog-faces in the foxholes, hoped that the Nazi regime would collapse soon, ending the war. Some held more pessimistic opinions, Wilcox among them. Tempered by his recent experience in the Netherlands, Wilcox wrote about it in his journal:

Monday, December 4, 1944. A Camp in Northern France.

Mom and Dad,

I decided to start another journal. This past Saturday I caught a ride into a French city near by, my first 24-hour pass in months. I bought this notebook in a run-down little shop there, the French version of the kind selling stationery, fountain pens, and business supplies. Between wartime shortages and looting by both departing Germans and French profiteers alike, little was available for sale. I used my high school French telling the shopkeeper what I was looking for. He stepped into the back and brought out this little leather-bound notebook. He said he'd salvaged it the other day while rummaging through his demolished storeroom.

We haggled about the price. I ended up paying him more than it was worth after I saw the gaunt appearance of his children. Kids have suffered a lot in this war, too much fear and never enough to eat. I gave them all the candy I had with me. I've never had my hands kissed by children before. I taught them how to give a good old-fashioned American handshake next time a friendly GI comes by.

I've missed having a journal, but I was reluctant to start another. Technically, I'm not supposed to carry any journal or diary with me into a combat zone, in case it falls into enemy hands. I obeyed that order in the past but lost my last journal while away fighting in Normandy. We left our extra gear behind in England under lock and key. (Back then, they told us we'd only be deployed a short time, but, as you now know, not everything in the invasion went according to plan.) When we finally returned to Britain weeks later, we found that rear echelon GI's, who supposedly guarded our belongings, had broken in and ransacked through everything. I hope whoever stole that other notebook enjoys reading it.

This time, I'm ignoring regulations. I almost hope this does fall into German hands. Maybe they'd see what a selfish, senseless, cruel war they've brought on others and themselves. They'd learn that this American soldier and thousands of others harbor no imperialistic or idealistic designs on Germany or its people. They'd read we all long to get this over and get back home.

We've been here in Northern France for a couple of days now resting and refitting after finally being pulled out of the Netherlands—another case of where the planners told us our deployment would last only days, but we stayed on through weeks and weeks of desperate fighting. The army gave us the first showers we'd had in almost two months. They issued us new uniforms (the smelly old ones near falling apart from constant wear in the Dutch dampness) and trucked us down to this camp.

We'd had a Thanksgiving meal of sorts a couple weeks ago, on the day thereof. The lukewarm meal in the field lacked much for giving thanks. Two days ago, the division served up another turkey dinner, this time with all the trimmings. We felt like the situation is truly improving. That feeling of comfort came with a price. The rest of the day and through the night all that rich, real food caused problems. Most of us came down with what Gramps used to call "the crab apple shuffle." (Without going into specifics, let me add that the latrines here are a medieval French design. At least I had a roof overhead and no one shooting at me when I used the facilities.) By this morning, my insides felt much better.

There's a credible rumor going around that our turn is coming soon for a leave in Paris. That would be nice. I personally doubt now that this war will be over by Christmas. "End the War in '44" has a nice ring to it, but that slogan's dying fast. The Germans demonstrated in Holland that they have an awful lot of fight left as we back them up to their own borders. I still hope I'll see Paris. Before the war is over or I return to the states, I want to tour the city and get a feel for its history. That would be a decent Christmas present if Uncle Sam wants to give me something short of sending me home.

I finally let them make me a sergeant. Nothing much changed. I'd been acting corporal leading another squad for over two months since Sgt. Houseman was killed early on during our last deployment. I used to think I'd stay out of leadership, but realities of survival have scoured such naïve ideas from my thinking. I've seen firsthand how cheap life is in a war, how foolishly wasted. I now want at least a little control over how my life and the lives of those I care about are put at risk.

Headquarters says we'll stay here in these old French Army barracks for a while. Some of the guys think it'll be until the good fighting weather comes in the spring. All I know is that the last operation chewed up the whole division. Coming back to full strength may take a while.

Anyway, we're out of danger for the time being. The hope of celebrating a Merry Christmas away from battle has already lifted our spirits some, but nothing fills the entire void left by those we buried back in Holland: Adair, Rostock, Shapiro, Houseman. Beauchamp and Lennox remain in the hospital. Navarre's wounds got him the golden ticket back to the states. Reynolds, a handful of others and I are about all that's left of the old training company that started out at jump school back in Georgia.

Wendell Burnanski is now part of my squad, another North Georgia jump school alumnus. He's a man of contradictions, both a well-known troublemaker and one of the best men to have around in combat. A bona fide hero, but he fell into deep hot water after coming out of Holland.

They talked me into taking him into my squad, sort of a last reprieve for him before they give up and drum him out entirely. Our battalion's commander thought, with my teaching background, I might be able to deal with him. I'm stuck with the situation for the time being.

We had our first active morning today since we reorganized the platoons. We've been out on drill already, did some calisthenics, and ran for five miles—all in the late autumn rain! They're pushing us to keep a fighting edge. After the combat we've seen, this jump-school stuff is a picnic. I'd gladly run in the cold rain all day if nobody's shooting at me. We're sitting around now before lunch drying out and killing time.

The Lieutenant strode into the building. He opened the inner door and stepped into the squad room. Cooper dropped the boots he was cleaning, whipped the toothpick out of his mouth as he stood and shouted, "'Ten-hut!"

(The Lieutenant figured they'd seen him coming the whole time, but aware of this game, played his part accordingly.)

The men immediately dropped personal tasks and stood at attention. Everyone except Private Wendell Burnanski. He continued upon his bunk, smoking his cigarette, a distant look in his eyes, no reaction to Cooper's shout. Not an accepted part of the game.

Wilcox couldn't let Burnanski embarrass his squad in front of their Lieutenant like this. He moved to lay into him. Cooper, who was closer, beat him to it, giving a quick, hard kick to a bedpost and a harsh whisper, "Ski! Straighten up!"

Burnanski snuffed out his cigarette in the ration can he used for an ashtray. He rolled off the bunk, and came slowly, sullenly, to attention. A bandage on his right cheekbone and a fresh scar above his left eyebrow gave him a menacing, primeval appearance.

"At ease," said the Lieutenant. The other men relaxed. Burnanski maintained his pose. The Lieutenant paused without looking in Burnanski's direction. Only a small inclination of his head hinted attention tuned that way. He spoke evenly and coolly, showing no hint of irritation in his voice, addressing the squad in his soft Carolina drawl. "Men, we're receiving some replacements today. More in the future. We need 'em bad. They'll have good enough training for regular infantry but not what they'll need to stay alive in the airborne or help our platoon by a long shot." He glanced from man to man as he spoke, looking each one in the eye, except Burnanski. "I know y'all are beat. I know y'all have done more than your fair share in this here war, but you've got to help me with the new men, for your sakes and theirs. Make 'em feel at home, part of the team. We'll be heading out on some field problems soon. Do whatever y'all can to bring 'em up to snuff. Their lives and your own depend on it in the next fight."

Puzzled by these comments, Wilcox thought, *What's with this pep talk? Not a good sign. This is only a small squad, and he's just a platoon leader. Will he perform junior officer theatrics before every squad in this platoon? Maybe something else is up.*

The Lieutenant paused again, looking the men over once more. He tersely added, "Burnanski, I want to talk with you." The Lieutenant jerked his head toward the door. "Outside!" He turned and walked from the room. Burnanski scowled and followed.

That's it, Wilcox thought. *It's for Burnanski's benefit. The Lieutenant only set the stage for the inevitable confrontation. He's not skirting the issue, but hitting it head on. Good deal!*

The Lieutenant led Burnanski out the entryway at a brisk pace. Tattered Wehrmacht orders of the day, still tacked to a corkboard, fluttered as they passed. Neither man said anything. They came out and headed around the far end of the building.

Wilcox ducked through the squad room's rear door and dashed down the narrow back hall to a battered desk in the corner. *After all,* he thought, *I'm Burnanski's squad leader. Let's see how the Lieutenant handles him.*

The cracked wooden chair wobbled as he stepped up onto it. From there he stepped to the desktop and grabbed onto a rafter beam. His lower back throbbed in protest, but he pulled himself up to roof level anyway. He clinging to the rafter, he could just manage to peer out through the cobwebs in the rows of small louvered openings where the roof met the wall. (For all their vaunted Germanic efficiency and attention to detail, the previous occupants had not made their French P.O.W. orderlies clean these dusty webs out.) Cool, fresh air blew in through the weathered slats. A welcome contrast to the damp laundry smells of the squad room.

A horizontal slice of the scene outside comprised Wilcox's field of vision through the slats. In that partial view, he saw Burnanski standing motionless on the damp ground facing toward the building. He had assumed the militarily correct stance for an enlisted man expecting a reprimand from a superior, and yet, being Burnanski, still conveyed a slight air of contempt.

The Lieutenant stood just out of Wilcox's restricted line of sight, beneath the louvered opening, and then he stepped into view. "At ease, Burnanski. Let's lay rank aside for a moment and talk man to man."

Burnanski did not relax. The "lay rank aside" and "man to man" expressions didn't faze him. He had received a half dozen lectures already, from the colonel and the appointed legal counsel on down to the chaplain and the stockade provost sergeant. Although Burnanski dropped out of high school and performed manual labor in a steel mill, he'd received exposure to a lot of psychology in an out of the army during past attempts to control his behavior. His attitude now seemed to say, "Don't bother, Lieutenant. Heard it before."

For a moment, the two tall men stood facing each other, the thinner, crisply dressed Lieutenant and bulk of Burnanski, casually dressed in rumpled O.D. jump pants and white T-shirt. Background noise seemed louder during the Lieutenant's pause: Water dripping off the roof and plopping onto the sodden ground below; road traffic rumbling in the distance; and a faint cadence call sounding from the parade ground.

The Lieutenant studied Burnanski for a moment. The officer took a breath and spoke evenly and directly despite Burnanski's unspoken refusal to open himself to what the Lieutenant would say. Wilcox realized now that his new platoon leader possessed some definite potential as a commander, who should never to speak down to a subordinate nor ever plead, even with the hard cases. The men under orders to obey him were Americans, citizen soldiers in a way the world hadn't seen before. They wanted respect as equals, even by a superior officer, even while being reprimanded, scolded, chewed-out. Not something every officer or non-com understood.

Without harshness or rancor, the Lieutenant firmly laid out what he wished to communicate. "Burnanski, I know you've heard some of this already from the Major, but I want you to know where you stand with me, as well. From your record, I see you've been a troublemaker from the beginning of your airborne career. Even before you came into the army, so I've heard. But in combat, you've been one of the best in this regiment, maybe the whole division, or used to be. We both know some brass wanted to do more than bust you back to private. They wanted to throw you to the wolves in a formal court martial, leave your hide moldering in a cell 'til doomsday. However, the Colonel let the Major, Captain and I stick our necks out for you one last time. You're out of the stockade and in my platoon and this squad. It's your last chance: Shape up now for the good of this squad and yourself.

"We've been through a lifetime of fightin' in Normandy and Holland. There's much more ahead because we're Airborne. We've lost too many good men. Nothing will ever bring 'em back. Ed Gluszcak was one of the best, but we have to put his death behind us. We must rebuild this platoon and make it effective again. We need the help of every 'old-timer' to do it. We owe it to the men we've lost to keep going. Gluszcak would tell you the same if he were here."

Burnanski stiffened more at each mention of Gluszcak's name. A loud engine rumble and a splashing of puddles announced several "deuce and a half" trucks coming down the road. The rising noise of their approach brought a temporary halt to the Lieutenant's talk with Burnanski.

The Lieutenant turned toward the traffic, so did Wilcox from his perch up in the corner of the barracks' back hallway. Wilcox could see a small stretch of the road as the first trucks rolled by. Canvas flaps of at the rear of each truck tied open, soldiers in fresh uniforms seated inside. Wilcox recognized them for what they were: *Replacements!* His eye twitched again.

Wilcox dropped down to the hallway floor and rubbed his lower back while the convoy passed outside. Replacements spelled trouble in the airborne divisions. The veterans had learned from experience that coming back up to full cadre meant redeployment in the near future. Wilcox had hoped the inevitable arrival of replacements would come in trickles, giving those recently returned from the combat front more time to recover. Whatever way replacements came, their arrival meant the old hands must tackle the uncomfortable task of teaching the new men what had caused the death of close friends and what might keep the new ones alive.

The roar of the truck engines decreased. Wilcox pulled himself back up to listen to Lieutenant and Burnanski again. The Lieutenant was already talking.

". . . hazed and abused replacements in the past," he said. "Driven 'em into the dirt. I won't let you do that in my platoon. We need 'em too much."

For all his heroics, everyone knew rough treatment of new men ranked high among Burnanski's past vices. Burnanski remained at attention the whole time. He spoke without looking at the Lieutenant, "I'm no longer a non-com. I'll do my own job, but I ain't babysittin' puppies anymore."

The Lieutenant put his fists on his hips and leaned forward. His eyes bored into Burnanski, but the big private never shifted under the pressure. "You've had your opportunity blowing off steam. Heaven knows, two guys from that bar fight are in the hospital right now, thanks to you. Save it for the Krauts. From now on, lay off the new men and help 'em over the hump 'til they're part of the team."

Burnanski remained unmoved by the Lieutenant's attempt to reason with him. With the slightest hint of irritation he said, "Is that *all*, sir?"

The Lieutenant leaned in, his eyes only inches from Burnanski's. He spoke in a cold voice just above a whisper, almost too soft for Wilcox to hear, "I've cut you a whole morning of slack. Now it's time to reel it in. Add my warning to what you heard from the Captain and the Major: Shape up, lay off and help out."

A long silence as the Lieutenant paused, his eyes still fixed on Burnanski's. The Lieutenant thrust at the heart of the situation and asked, "Do you even *want* to be here?"

The Lieutenant had asked a key question, so obvious that nobody had hit on it before in dealing with Burnanski. He'd touched a raw personal nerve. Burnanski's defiant expression wavered as he struggled with a thrust no amount of hard bluster could parry. The fog of both men's breath hung in the chilly air. The Lieutenant let Burnanski ponder things a few heartbeats more, then leaned back and said crisply, "Dismissed." He waited for Burnanski's salute, returned it smartly, then wheeled about and picked his way carefully through the mud around the building back to the waiting jeep.

Burnanski continued to stand outside, his face a contorted mixture of doubt, rage, and confusion. After the Lieutenant's jeep had started up, splashed through another puddle, and drove away, he shuddered and slowly felt around his pockets for another cigarette, lighted one and snapped the match away. He took one long drag, turned and stalked back around to the barracks' entrance, his dark face hardening back into a scowl.

CHAPTER TWO

Wilcox

An uncomfortable silence fell upon the stuffy room when Wilcox hurried back and leaned by the window with journal and pencil again.

Burnanski jerked the front door open and slammed it behind himself. Acknowledging no one in the room, he swung himself up, flopped back onto his bunk. The wood creaked in protest. He returned to staring at the ceiling. The other men continued cleaning their equipment as if the Lieutenant had never come and Burnanski's insolent return routinely occurred.

Wilcox attempted writing some more but gave it up. He walked over and lay on his bunk. He now had a lot more to think about, thoughts he knew he'd have to consider eventually, but he'd hoped it would have been later than this. He wondered at first about Burnanski and war's awful devastation of good men. This line of thinking never led to satisfactory conclusions—bitter aspects of human conflict forever beyond reason.

Wilcox's mind drifted over to the imminent prospect of receiving replacements. Although he needed them, something within him also dreaded their arrival. He reflected for a moment on the natural tendency of veterans to ignore new men, distance themselves. He knew this tendency grew out of a harsh fact of combat life and death, a stark chain of logic: A) New men made mistakes; B) Mistakes in combat cost lives; C) Because they made mistakes, combat usually killed new men first. Therefore, veterans tended to avoid replacements because D) New men could get you killed; and E) If you didn't get to know new men, their abrupt departures affected your emotions less. Within himself and within his new squad, Wilcox now must fight this reasoning. He must push himself and the veterans to accept the new men and teach them survival skills based on real combat experience, going beyond the manuals and maneuvers they had drilled and operated under in previous training. However, to survive was not enough.

Although one of the lowliest denominations among infantry units, he must forge his small squad into an effective team to fight and win in battle. This required a commitment of physical and mental energy the veterans had in short supply and development of unspoken trust within the unit.

"Reynolds is coming," reported Vincenti, who had informally taken over the watch from Wilcox. "He's leading a buncha guys this way. They're carrying a lotta gear."

"Replacements," Wilcox said with resignation, coming over for a look himself. He thought, *I'd hoped for a couple more days of rest before becoming a den mother. The Lieutenant knew ours were on their way when he gave us the pep talk.*

"Why can't they let some other platoon have 'em?" muttered Friedenfeld, joining them at the window.

"At least we got somebody now to fetch coal for the stoves," said Cooper, "and clean the latrines."

Sergeant First Class Bill Reynolds appeared outside, leading several green-looking troopers. Beyond Wilcox's window, the sergeant stopped the group and looked the men over and their weapons. He checked his clipboard, pointed at two of the men, and gestured at the decorated barracks door. Even through the window, Wilcox could hear Reynolds booming voice directing the men. "You 'n you, in there. Rest of you wait right here."

Reynolds led the two men toward the door. One of the new men seemed bewildered by the sergeant's quick directions, things happening too fast for him. The other fumbled with his gear, gawking at the Christmas decorations as they stepped into the doorway.

Reynolds strode in on his long legs, grinning wide and leading the two replacements. Reynolds towered over the new men (like Burnanski and some others, he had circumvented the maximum height regulation for paratroopers). He spoke to the existing squad with a mock formality, "Gentlemen, I just picked up some new men for your squad, young'uns fresh off the boat and full of vitamins, eager to prove themselves worthy of our outfit. I present Privates Nurnberg and Tobin."

Burnanski turned away on his bunk, cursing softly to himself.

Wilcox looked the new men over himself. *So young,* he thought. *Have to be last year's high school grads.* Nurnberg, the bewildered one, was of average height and medium build, with short blond hair, receding slightly. His nervous smile flickered back and forth between a grin and a smirk. Tobin was short and stocky with black hair slicked straight back. He also grinned nervously, revealing a pair of large buckteeth.

Before anyone said anything more, Sgt. Herdlika, Wilcox's counterpart from 1st Squad next door on the hall, stuck his head into the room and called to Reynolds. "Hey, Sarge, here's another one for 2nd Squad. Lieutenant sent him over special. He's a machine gunner."

Well, Wilcox thought, *for all the trouble they're going to be, this last bit's at least some welcome news.* Rifles comprised his squad's main weaponry, but typical airborne squads also included a .30 caliber light machine gun. This differed from regular infantry, which used the Browning Automatic Rifle as a squad automatic weapon. Airborne strategists considered the B.A.R. too long and heavy, since it couldn't be broken down for parachute drop. Headquarters hadn't assigned Wilcox's new squad a machine gun crew yet.

"In here, kid," Herdlika said to someone in the entryway as he stepped back out of the room.

"Thanks, Sarge." The third replacement stepped into the room. The squad saw the smiling face of a lean, light-haired private, probably another 19-year old, his gear slung over one shoulder, his personal carbine slung over the other.

"And who might you be, my fine man?" boomed Reynolds. Wilcox hated his evident cheerfulness in the misery he knowingly inflicted on the veterans.

"Anderson, Joseph W.," replied the newest man. Like the other two new men, he was only two or three years younger than most of the veterans in age, but months of combat experience made them appear so much older now. So fresh, he seemed even younger than the other two new men.

"Gentlemen, this is your new home." Reynolds gestured around the room. "Meet your squad leader, Sergeant Wilcox, his assistant, Corporal Cooper. Those are Privates Friedenfeld n' Vincenti, and that's Burnanski up on the bunk." The squad nodded or waved a hand at the mention of their names. Burnanski didn't turn his face away from the wall. Reynolds nodded again at Wilcox. "Take 'em under your wing. Got some other guys to drop off."

"Right, Sarge," Wilcox said and stepped forward. Inside he groaned as old "first day of school" feelings flashed through him and passed on. *Here goes nothing,* he thought.

Friedenfeld and Vincenti quickly slipped out the door, temporarily avoiding contact with the new men. Cooper stayed behind, because he was assistant squad leader and because he was a barrack room comedian with a new audience for his jokes. Burnanski ignored everyone from the sanctity of his bunk, but Wilcox knew that as squad leader he had to crank up his energy and make a show of being friendly himself. "Wilcox, Anthony P.," He said, forcing himself to smile and extend a hand. "Call me Sarge, Wilcox, Tony, or 'Professor,' though mostly we go by last names around here, like the rest of the army."

The tallest of the three shook Wilcox's hand first. "Nurnberg, Manfred C. Folks call me 'Manny.'" Large hands but a tenuous grip.

The second man, shortest of the three, spoke, "Tobin, William B. Folks call me 'Bucky.'"

For obvious dental reasons, Wilcox thought. *Strong grip, maybe that's good.*

"Anderson, Joseph P. Call me Joe," the newest man, the machine gunner, said with a friendly smile, firmly grasping the offered hand, looking Wilcox straight in the eye. "Why 'Professor?'"

Wilcox kept up the friendly effort, swallowing his cautious annoyance a bit. "Because I used to be a history teacher," he said.

"At *girls'* school, a private *girls'* school," added Cooper. Wilcox had played into one of his favorite routines.

"This is Henry H. Cooper. Call him 'Hank' or 'Coop,' and pay him no mind when he jokes about my teaching days," Wilcox said. "He always makes it sound like I worked in a harem or something. Raphoe Academy is a small, private girls' boarding school in Pennsylvania. My parents are administrators. That's the only way the board allowed a single guy like me on the faculty."

"Up to his eyeballs in debutantes and heiresses," sighed Cooper, rolling his eyes up at the imagined beauty of Wilcox's students.

"Braces and acne too," Wilcox added. He had warmed up as much as he could stomach into his squad leader role now and gave the new guys a nudge toward making the squad their home. "Take any open bunk, except that one." He nodded at the vacant bed beneath Burnanski. "Stow your gear and stand by. We're waiting for chow call."

"Good. I'm hungry," Tobin said.

"Same here," said Nurnberg.

Wilcox sat back down on his bunk and observed the new men. The old-timers had already occupied the two sets of bunks nearest the room's only source of heat. Friedenfeld and Vincenti roosted on one side, Cooper and Wilcox on the other. Two sets of empty bunks and the bottom of Burnanksi's set were vacant. Eyeing Burnanski, Nurnberg and Tobin prudently decided on sharing the next set of bunks on Cooper and Wilcox's side of the room. Anderson took the bottom bunk of the set opposite Burnanski's perch. Anderson sat on the bunk, testing its mattress.

"Careful of those bunks, boys," Wilcox cautioned.

"Yeah," added Cooper. "The guys who slapped 'em together ought to be slapped themselves."

"Inspect your bed slats," Wilcox continued. "P.O.W.'s cut them. Some boards have knots and break easily. Friedenfeld burst through onto Vincenti the first night here. And you'll want to check the stuffing in your mattress covers for lumps, too. Local farmers graciously supplied the U.S. Army with hay full of burs and thistles."

"Thistle makes me whistle," said Cooper. He gave a "wolf whistle" as he rose and started tucking in his shirt. "My sixth sense tells me it's about chow call time."

"His gut keeps better time than an Elgin watch," Wilcox said, grabbing on his own shirt from the line. It was still a little damp, but he put it on anyway. "Leave your gear. Grab your mess kits, gentlemen. Let's go!"

Cooper's uncanny sense of mealtime proved itself again. As they jogged from the barracks in the direction of the mess hall, the call sounded for the company's midday meal.

The veterans, mired in the Netherlands for weeks and weeks under British command, had subsisted on the unfamiliar fare that the Tommys supplied, so American-style food, even canned B-ration stuff, provided a welcome change from British field rations with their tinned bully beef, oxtail soup, and Yorkshire pudding. There was no need to explain to the new men the need to hurry. They'd been in the army long enough to know that those who got in line first usually got better helpings and the possibility of seconds if any worth having.

Jump boots tromped through the wet grass, and mess kits clattered, as they approached the tents. A few other men already formed up, and scores converged. Wilcox jostled his way into the line with Cooper shepherding the new men in-between them.

The division had swamped the existing mess facilities on site, those intact or repairable, so each battalion erected additional mess areas. Their unit's slap-dash mess hall consisted of several large O.D. field tents pitched together on the edge of what used to be a lawn beside some utility buildings. Field kitchen vehicles set up beside one of the buildings. The adjacent tents provided sit-down dining and a lecture hall between meal times. Sheets of plywood nailed onto sawhorses served as tables. Rough plank benches provided seating. Recent rains and hundreds of tramping jump boots had already churned up the grass and exposed a large patch of mud. Straw and sawdust kept the mud in check. The tents smelled of fresh cut pine, raw earth, and stale coffee.

"Hey, Billy Yank!" a nearby voice shouted.

Wilcox turned and saw the grinning face of Sgt. Houston Avery, a couple places ahead of him, leaning out of the line and looking his way. Avery led a squad in a brother platoon and hailed from rural Georgia.

"Hey, Johnny Reb," Wilcox said, looking away, appearing to be busy with something, hoping Avery would leave him alone right now. Back in June, they'd once spent an artillery-filled night together crouched in a captured slit trench. Not much sleeping that night. They got to talking and somehow determined that their great-grandfathers had faced each other across the Wheatfield at Gettysburg over eighty years before.

Avery was friendly enough, a good enough fighting man, but his particular thick-tongued way of speaking grated on Wilcox. Wilcox described it as "a Southern drawl spoken with a mouth full of golf balls." It presented difficulties in understanding what Avery was saying, and Avery invariably butchered Wilcox's name.

"Hey, Wheel-cock, got ya some new cannon fodder?" He asked, nodding at the new men behind him in line.

"Yeah, just in." Wilcox turned away hoping he wouldn't have more of Avery's jabber penetrating his train of thought.

"Babes in arms," Avery persisted. "They don' make 'em like they used ta."

"I hope you get some too," Wilcox said. "Real soon."

"Got mine already," Avery said, jerking his head at three skinny greenhorns standing ahead of him in line. "All of 'em Yankees too! Reckon mah vacation's ovah before it starts."

The bored cooks slopped Spam, canned green beans, re-hydrated potatoes and canned peaches on the mess trays, ladling thin brown gravy over everything. *Watch the peaches!* No bread; only hard G.I. crackers. *Little changed from the hardtack of the Civil War eighty years before,* Wilcox thought. *Surely, this isn't surplus from that era. At least there's some coffee!* Over all, no five-star fare—even the best army food never matched what the school dining room served up back home. However, it was definitely an American-style menu, with reassuring familiarity in its mundane contents.

Wilcox led his new men through those already seated toward an empty plywood table. They set their food down and began eating. After a few mouthfuls, Cooper's elbow jabbed Wilcox's side. Cooper nodded across the table. Nurnberg and Tobin looked askance at Anderson seated between them, his head bowed in prayer.

Anderson's quiet action, a godly intrusion into the unsanctified atmosphere of the raucous mess tent, aroused Wilcox's concerns for his squad. The private meditation ran contrary to his army experience. Fine for civilians praying in a mom-and-pop diner, or the occasional Catholic soldier casually making the sign of the cross, but earnest public display of religion often spelled trouble in the army he'd come to know. He feared this exposed only the tip of an iceberg with Anderson. *Great,* he thought, *just great! Some kind of religious nut on my hands, and he seemed to be the sharper one!*

Others in the squad sat transfixed, tin mess cups in hand or gravy dripping from poised forks, while Anderson completed his personal blessing. The hubbub of the mess tent continued in the background. Men talking, laughing, steel utensils scrapping on tins. Anderson raised his head. An awkward moment of silence lingered before others turned eyes away and resumed eating.

Avery leaned back from the table behind Wilcox and rasped in his ear, "One of yours still needs weanin'."

Wilcox flushed with irritation. Avery had stated the obvious: He didn't need some Sunday School boy slowing down the development of the new squad. *Great! Just great!* He thought again. *Have to keep a special eye on this Holy Joe.* Weariness flooded over him. He gulped his coffee, burning his tongue.

"It's been a long time since I saw a man give thanks for Spam," he said, breaking the strained lack of conversation at his table, trying to sound friendly. Anderson smiled, nodded his head once, and continued eating. The others remained silent.

Thoughts pricked at Wilcox's conscience for his judgmental reaction to the replacement's prayer. He'd known some malnourished boys in basic training. Those young men came from depression-ravaged homes, sometimes no home at all. Food had been scarce. Such simple fare as today's would be a bounty. Wilcox thought, *Maybe this new kid's seen difficulty in his background too.* Philosophical thorns stabbed his conscience further:

Regardless of this kid's background, free expression is part of what we're fighting for, he reminded himself.

"Know why they call it 'Spam,' don't ya?" asked Cooper, breaking the interlude with the lame old joke.

"I think its name comes from them making it out of shoulder pork and ham," ventured Tobin, who hadn't heard this one before. "That's what the radio commercials say."

"Nah," said Cooper, setting up for the punch line. "It's from the sound it makes when an army cook flings it onto your plate."

Tobin grinned at the small joke, showing his prominent teeth again.

A friendly enough start, Wilcox thought. *Sooner we get to know the new men, the better for the new squad.* He swallowed his mouthful and asked a standard "get-acquainted" question. "Where all you guys from?"

"Palo Alto, California," said Tobin. "It's near 'Frisco."

"Heard of it," Wilcox said. "Stanford University's there, isn't it?"

"Yeah," said Tobin. "My older brothers are both grads. I'm hoping to enroll there too, maybe play ball for 'em after the war."

"What kind of ball?" asked Cooper.

"Mainly baseball," said Tobin, wiping gravy from his chin.

"Really? What position?" Cooper asked, crumbling crackers into his gravy.

"Shortstop," said Tobin.

Cooper nodded at Wilcox. "The professor here played right field for Penn State."

"On the rare occasions away from the lumber business," Wilcox added.

"What does that mean?" Nurnberg asked.

"Old baseball slang. Means gathering splinters from sittin' on the bench," Cooper explained.

"I knew that one," Tobin said.

Cooper said, "Played a littler catcher myself, on our company's team back in England."

"You guys got a team now?" asked Tobin. "When can I try out?"

"Probably after Christmas," Wilcox said, "If we stay around in camp that long. Ranks are thin, so there's room for you, but everybody's thinking football right now. Headquarters wants us to scrape a couple of teams together. They'll play before the whole division on Christmas Day. Baseball's taken back seat for a while. Any of you guys play football?"

"I also did in high school," said Nurnberg.

"So did I," said Anderson.

"Me too," said Tobin.

"Well, I'll let the Lieutenant know," Wilcox said. "He's helping to round up talent for the teams."

Friedenfeld and Vincenti plopped down a short distance away, still enjoying the luxury of ignoring the new men. Wilcox kept the question and answer session going. "How 'bout you? 'Nergberg,' is it? Where are you from?"

"*Nurn*-berg," he corrected. "Originally 'Von Nürnberg,' but Ellis Island changed it when they processed my grandfather. I'm from West Milwaukee, Wisconsin. It's west of--"

"Milwaukee!" chimed Cooper.

"Of course," Nurnberg said.

"Wisconsin, 'Land of Beer and Cheese,' isn't it?" Wilcox asked.

"Yeah," Nurnberg said. "That's the place."

"Hey! Anyone in your family happen to work in a brewery?" asked Cooper suddenly showing a more than mild interest. "Your folks ever send you any packages?"

"Sorry, no brewery," answered Nurnberg. "There's more to the Milwaukee area than beer and cheese."

"Like what?" asked Cooper as if nothing else could be of any importance.

"Like motorcycles," said Nurnberg. "My dad and uncle build 'em at the Harley-Davidson plant. Ever heard of 'Harleys?'"

"Good bikes," said Cooper, his interest in Nurnberg becoming a slight bit real. "Like they say, 'If you can't brew beer, build a motorcycle.'"

"I'm not sure that's an actual expression," said the clueless Tobin.

"If it ain't, it oughta be," Cooper replied. "Before I became a trooper, I thought of going into the M.P.'s just so I could ride their 'cycles.'" He turned toward Friedenfeld, "Hey, Rodeo! Got a guy here from Milwaukee named 'Nerdbug.'"

"'*Nurn-berg*,'" Nurnberg corrected.

Friedenfeld asked, "Sprechen Sie Deutsch?"

"Ja, die ganze Zeit zu Hause," said Nurnberg. "Meine Großeltern kamen aus der alten Heimat vor dem letzten Krieg. Und Sie?"

"Mein Opa war ein Wolgadeutscher, der auszog, Wyoming kam," said Friedenfeld. "Aber Meine Oma war von den Deutschen, die in Victoria, Texas."

"What's all the Jerry-jabber about?" Cooper asked. "All I caught was 'Wyoming' and 'Victoria, Texas.'"

"Told him I spoke German at home," Nurnberg said, "and that my grandparents came from Germany before the last war."

"And I told him my grandpa was a Volga German who came out to Wyoming," said Friedenfeld.

"All Germans are vulgar," Vincenti said.

"As much as all Italians are idiots," Friedenfeld shot back. "As I was saying before rudely interrupted, I told him my grandma's from German settlements down in Texas."

"Great!" complained Vincenti. "More Krauts in the company!"

"Better than another Eye-talian!" said Friedenfeld.

"Not the way I look at it," said Vincenti.

"Wise up," said Friedenfeld. "A third of Americans have German ancestry."

"Tobin's French, but I'm Italian on my mom's side," said Tobin. "Her maiden name was *Capraio*."

"*Paisan!* Someone with a good pedigree for a change!" said Vincenti, reaching across and shaking Tobin's hand.

Burnanski came to the table, sat at the farthest end, acknowledging no one in the group, and began eating in a mechanical sort of way.

Everyone fell silent for a moment. Even the new men sensed something about him that said, "*Leave this one alone.*"

Wilcox again forced himself to continue with the question, picking things up again. He asked, "How 'bout you, Anderson, where you from?"

Anderson smiled his disarming smile again. "I'm from Glen Ellyn, Illinois. It's a village west of Chicago, about a 45-minute train ride away."

Wilcox shot Burnanski a quick glance to see if he'd heard the reference to Chicago. Burnanski came from Gary, Indiana, the steel mill town on Lake Michigan southeast of Chicago, but either Burnanski hadn't heard or didn't care.

"Where are you from?" asked Anderson, turning the tables on Wilcox.

"I'm from Manheim, Pennsylvania. It's a small town outside of nowhere," he said.

"Except for the girl's school," Cooper chimed in.

"Cooper always has girls on his mind," Wilcox said.

"Only when I ain't thinking 'bout women," corrected Cooper.

"Cooper," Wilcox explained, "if you haven't guessed from his dialect, is from Brooklyn."

"It's a large town inside of New York City," Cooper said, getting up from his seat. "Anybody wanna try for seconds?" Nurnberg and Tobin got up and tagged after him to see what the cooks might let them have.

Anderson and Wilcox sat silently for a moment, busy with their food. The background hubbub of other diners filled the void. Friedenfeld and Vincenti argued about popular music, which big band was better, Glen Miller's or Benny Goodman's. Burnanski drank his coffee and lit a cigarette.

Wilcox compelled himself to think about challenges and obstacles with the new men, determining to work everyone, new hands and old, even Burnanski, somehow into a team. *Easier at the beginning, back in Georgia and in England,* he thought. Back then, everyone was new, all forged in the same fire of harsh early training. All honed together as a fighting force in England. However, Normandy shattered that superb team. Welded back together, Holland shattered it worse. *Have to patch things together once more,* he thought. *Lives might depend on how well I patch them.*

Anderson rose from the table, interrupting Wilcox's thoughts.

"Excuse me, I'm heading on back."

"Sure. I'll be along in a few minutes." Wilcox replied.

Friedenfeld and Vincenti also got up, leaving Wilcox with Burnanski, who sat staring off into the distance. Burnanski snuffed out his cigarette butt in the gravy on his tray and lit another. *Well*, Wilcox thought, *what'll happen if Holy Joe collides with Burnanski? Better keep on my toes about that. Someone might get hurt, and won't be Burnanski!*

CHAPTER THREE

Cooper

After lunch, the squad gathered with their platoon and others beneath the mess tent again. K.P.'s had cleared tables to the rear and lined benches in rows toward the front. The battalion intelligence officer droned on in a lecture about the current state of the war. He used a crude map on a chalkboard to show how Operation Market-Garden the division had recently been a part of in Holland fit into the overall big picture of the European Theater. He explained the progress of Allied strategy, with major thrusts toward Germany from the British and Canadian armies through Holland toward the industrial Ruhr Valley in the north and the American and French armies toward the Saarland in the south. In passing, he pointed out a quiet sector in the forested Ardennes upland region in between.

A restless tension grew during this lecture time. For the new replacements, sitting around there deflated the excitement and stress of arriving at their new units that morning. Anxious to prove themselves, they wanted action not chalk talks. For the veterans, who in these situations usually fought urges to fall asleep after lunch, the lecture revealed a disturbing reality: All their bloody efforts of the past months in the north helping the British thrust had amounted to little significant change in the strategic picture. Because Market-Garden's big gamble came up short, millions of Dutch people remained under occupation, facing bitter reprisals, worse oppressions and harsh restrictions. Even Cooper, no student of history like Wilcox, concluded in hindsight that the Netherlands operation had squandered men, equipment and supplies that would have better aided Patton or one of the other commanders pressing to the south and east.

As the briefing dragged on, a strong hunch grew within Cooper about the Allied war effort in Western Europe losing energy, slowing down, stalling on a broad front as cold weather and snow approached, showing definite signs of settling in for the winter. *Spells trouble for the Airborne,* he thought. *Come spring, we'll likely have to jump-start the drive by jumpin' behind the Jerries. In the meantime, Krauts won't be idle. What are Kraut plans for winter? Are they as worn out as we are? Will I ever see Paris?*

Mail call followed the lecture. A bright moment in a thus-far dull afternoon. Friedenfeld returned to the barracks with an armful of small partially opened parcels. He dumped them on his bed and moaned. "It's happening again,"

"Burr under your saddle, Cowboy?" asked Vincenti.

"What's that on your bed?" Cooper asked. "Bricks wrapped in brown paper?"

"Fruitcakes!" said Friedenfeld. "More fruitcakes! Why can't it be razor blades or long underwear or something useful? Last December in training camp stateside, friends and relatives from Texas, Nebraska and Wyoming sent me over a dozen fruitcakes for Christmas. I got so sick of 'em. Tried to give them away, but had few takers. I buried the rest at Fort Benning."

"Looks like they've come back from the grave and followed you overseas," Vincenti said.

"Any of you new guys care for some fruitcake?" Friedenfeld asked.

"No thank you," said Anderson.

"None for me, thanks," said Tobin.

Nurnberg said, "I'm still full from lunch."

"Well, if any of you changes your mind," Friedenfeld said, "they'll be here tomorrow."

"And the next day," said Vincenti.

"And the next day," said Cooper.

Later in the afternoon, Cooper lounged on his bunk. No slacker, as hard working as any of the farm boys when action required it, his big city instincts and army experience taught him energy conservation whenever possible. He picked his teeth with a homemade toothpick, casually observing the replacements stowing away their equipment. Nurnberg and Tobin opened duffels and started spreading their socks and underwear out on their bunks. *Mommy taught you good, boys*, Cooper chuckled to himself.

Cooper raised his head to get a better view of Anderson's activity. Anderson, as a machine gunner, had been issued an M-1 carbine as a personal weapon, shorter and lighter than the standard M-1 infantry rifle. He looked his carbine over, inspecting for dirt and checking the action.

Sign of good breedin' in my book, thought Cooper. *Baby that thing. Your piece should be your most treasured earthly possession. Take care of it; it'll take care of you.* "How many jumps you new guys had?" Cooper asked all the new men aloud.

"Five stateside," answered Nurnberg.

"Same here," said Tobin.

"Me too," said Anderson.

Barely qualified, thought Cooper. *All of 'em.* "What about in England?" he asked.

"None for me there," said Nurnberg.

"Me neither," said Tobin.

Cooper and Wilcox exchanged a brief glance.

This ain't good, Cooper thought. *Five jumps stateside minimum to qualify for paratrooper's jump wings.* He thought about his own experience: Less than 20% of his training company passed the rigors of jump school and earned their wings. Intense airborne infantry training followed, plus several additional jumps stateside. Once in England, there had been a series of daylight and night time practice jumps, constant drilling and field problems specific in preparation for the Invasion. The new guys couldn't be half as prepared for real combat. *The army's rushin' these guys to us wet behind the ears*, he thought. "How about you, Anderson?" he asked.

"I had one extra jump onto Salisbury Plain," said Anderson. "A quick demonstration they scraped together for the press and some visiting dignitaries."

In addition to basic infantry training they had before shipping over to the Continent, the division's training unit back in England should have also given the new men some advanced instruction in airborne combat techniques. "You guys had any combat trainin' before you got here?" Cooper asked.

"What we got in regular infantry school and only a couple weeks of airborne training in England," Nurnberg said. "The division training staff were preparing to ship over here when we came through, so we missed out on most of what they'd been doing in the weeks before we got there."

"They gave us some refresher training on various team weapons, like machine guns, mortars, bazookas," said Anderson, "but no field exercises."

"Mostly they put us to work packing up their stuff and loading it in trucks," added Tobin. "Said we'd catch up on other training after we got over here."

Only Cooper heard Wilcox's low groan.

Just peachy, thought Cooper. *Not many jumps, little extra training. Just dumped on us! Where'll the Captain and the Lieutenant begin? Where'll Wilcox? Where'll I?*

Cooper knew it would be murder to send these replacements into combat as they were. They had to be prepared, as much as possible in the haste of fighting the war. Ideally, the new men must learn more than mere survival. They needed to develop resourcefulness, exercising personal initiative, because anything could, and often did, go wrong in actual combat drops. Everyone needed cross-training in handling everyone else's job and weapons if need be. A dozen men might find themselves completing a mission for their entire platoon or even their whole company. It happened during those chaotic first 72 hours in Normandy. It could happen again.

What training they received back in the states provided only an introduction, a scratching of the surface of what an airborne assault required. The Major, Captain and the Lieutenant would initiate additional training in the broad sense. Non-coms like Reynolds, Cooper and Wilcox would drill in the finer details wherever possible. *Hopefully, there'll be enough time here in camp for the vets to hammer into the rookies some hard-earned lessons from this war,* Cooper thought. *Might save a few lives and make the squad an effective unit at the same time.*

Nurnberg and Tobin still sorted laundry. After stowing his own clothing and equipment, Anderson picked up his carbine again, disassembling and reassembling it without looking, a skill he might need in a foxhole some dark night. *Good boy,* thought Cooper as he continued to watch. *This new church-going guy shows some potential as a fightin' man.*

"It's good to have a home at last," Anderson said, looking up and seeing Cooper watching him. "Being a replacement is a life of uncertainty."

"Been there," Cooper replied. "Know it's a lot worse for new guys heading for the regular infantry. They herd 'em around like cattle. Send 'em to the front with no extra combat training. Get 'em killed 'n nobody even knows their names. Should get ta know you some here, and give you the training you shoulda got in England, before we see any fighting. We're suppos'ta be here at least 'til after Christmas. The way the war's windin' down for winter, maybe even 'til spring."

"Sounds good," Anderson said. "Building teamwork takes time."

"Sounds like an 'edgy-cated' person's answer," said Cooper. "Got any 'edgy-cation?'"

"A year of college. I joined up right after my second semester," Anderson said.

"I'm an 'edgy-cated' man myself," said Cooper, leaning back and putting his hands behind his head.

"Yeah," Wilcox said, picking up the conversation, "the school of hard knocks."

"'Tis true, 'tis true," lamented Cooper, "'Tis sad, but true."

"Actually, Cooper's smarter than he looks," Wilcox said. "He's our resident sports expert. Used to work concessions at Dodger games."

"Folks called me 'Ol' Peanuts, Popcorn, n' Cracker-Jack Cooper,'" he said, sticking in another toothpick and lying back on his bunk.

"We have a truce going between Cooper and Vincenti," Wilcox explained. "Normally, the Dodgers and Phillies are arch rivals."

"Yeah," said Cooper. "No baseball arguments for the present. Both teams' quality is down while key players serve in the war."

"Not worth the trouble," Vincenti said. "War's affecting college teams too."

Cooper asked Anderson, "Kid, what did ya study in college? You a history nut like the perfesser here?"

"I love history," Anderson said, "but I was studying for the ministry."

As if a silent bomb had gone off in the room, Cooper's astonished mouth lost control of his toothpick. It fell back into his throat. He sat up and coughed it out to avoid choking. Everyone else's eyeballs clicked on Joe Anderson. Even Burnanski flinched at the revelation.

Cooper cleared his throat to be sure the toothpick fully dislodged and asked hoarsely, "A ministerial student?"

"Why are you in the Army?" asked Tobin.

"Yeah," added Friedenfeld, leaning by the window, "you could've received a deferment and stayed out of this mess."

Anderson nodded, "I prayed about that. When my number came up, I knew God wanted me to go, so I didn't wait for an induction notice. I enlisted and volunteered for the airborne after infantry school."

"You're crazy, kid," shot Vincenti. He rolled over and picked up a copy of *Stars and Stripes*.

Cooper stood up, spread his arms and gestured around at the entire division about them, "But the Airborne?"

Wilcox said what everyone else thought: "Men die just training for this."

Cooper picked up his fallen toothpick and pointed it at Anderson. "As a ministerial student, you might've become a chaplain's assistant n' had a soft ride."

Anderson said simply, "I prayed about that too, but I believe the Lord has work of some kind for me right here with a combat unit."

Too much for Burnanski's ears, he slid off his bed and stalked out of the room. His typical rough method of closing the door shook the walls.

"Groan! 'Ski shoulda been the tester in a door factory!" Cooper said, shaking his head and inserting a new toothpick. *This Anderson guy's truly different.* Thinking of something to break the momentary silence and maybe change the subject, he asked, "Um, how do you like being a machine gunner?"

"I prayed about which weapon I'd be issued. I've gotten used to its quirks. Suits me just fine," Anderson said.

Cooper began coughing as he almost choked on his toothpick again. He rolled over on his stomach, reducing chances of a third incident. *Prayed about it too? Is this kid for real?* He thought. Cooper had never come across anything like this in the city or the army. No one so transparently straightforward and religiously sincere. Hard for him to fathom.

Vincenti turned a page and adjusted his newspaper. "Seem to pray about a lotta things, kid."

Anderson smiled, trying to set them at ease. "I'm just a born-again Christian. I try to pray about everything I can."

Cooper stared at Anderson in wonder. "Everything?"

"Well, it's what the Bible says, 'giving thanks always for all things.' So I pray about the important things, and sometimes the not-so-important, when they come to mind." Anderson leaned back with one elbow on his government-issue blanket, unembarrassed by what he told about himself, speaking with a calm conviction Cooper had never seen in anyone before. "I want God's will for my life. I've prayed about which service to join, which branch to enter, which weapon to use, which unit I'd be sent to."

Cooper glanced at Wilcox, shrugged, and turned toward to Anderson, "Well, kid, I've seen a lot in the short time I've been in this man's army, but you're truly somethin' different! Never thought of this outfit as someone else's answer to a prayer."

Wilcox echoed the thought. "From a candid observer's viewpoint," he said, "it's going to be interesting to see how someone like you fits in."

CHAPTER FOUR

Cooper

A field problem seemed in store for them during the coming night, the way Cooper figured. Wilcox guessed it too. The training schedule progressed quickly. A field exercise would expose the new men to large group airborne operations and expose weaknesses in the men themselves. Previous airborne strategy centered on the concept of "Air Envelopment," which involved dropping troopers behind enemy lines. This often came under the cover of darkness, like during the Normandy Invasion. A night problem seemed next on the training agenda.

"I'm going to have a talk with the other squad leaders," Wilcox told him. "I'm too keyed-up to lie around. Maybe Herdlika or the others have some ideas for working in the new men."

Cooper tried cautioning the others to get some rest. Nobody took him seriously. Most of the squad joined a mess tent crowd watching Bing Crosby, Bob Hope and Dorothy Lamour in a repeat showing of Paramount Pictures' *Road to Morocco*.

Cooper thought, *Seen that flick so much, I got parts of the dialog memorized. Bing: "We must storm the palace." Bob: "You storm. I'll stay here and drizzle." As for me, I'll stay here try for a nap.*

Only Anderson had remained behind, quietly writing a few letters and reading some kind of small leather-bound book.

Guess "Reverend Anderson" doesn't go to movies anyway, Cooper thought. *A little night problem might be just what Holy Joe needs.*

39

A typical night problem encompassed a nighttime field training exercise with predetermined objectives, like overland movement and practice assault on some position. Cooper could imagine the process leading to one being ordered: Before heading stateside for a conference, the General would've wasted no time shifting his division from field operations to implementing a concentrated training program preparing new men for combat. He'd confer with the regimental commanders about forging the reorganized and reinforced elements of the regiments into an efficient fighting force. The Colonel would meet with his staff about giving directives to the various battalions' headquarters. After receiving the directives, the Major would have his battalion operations officers dust off training manuals and plans leftover from their last stay in England. From those plans, orders for a night problem would go down to the company commanders. The Captain would call in the Lieutenant and the other platoon leaders and work out their units' roles for the coming night problem. The Lieutenant would turn to Reynolds, the platoon sergeant, who would do the dirty work of waking up the men. Having tried to warn the others, Cooper rested and awaited the inevitable. *"Sure as shootin' a night problem's coming,* he thought. *Feel it in my bones.*

The squad trickled back to the room before lights out. Nurnberg and Tobin thought the movie was hilarious, evidently never seeing it stateside or in England. A third-time viewing for Vincenti and Friedenfeld, but it still tickled them how much one of the camels resembled Sgt. Atmoore, a strutting drill instructor they'd suffered under back in the states.

Wilcox spent the evening playing chess in the NCO club and listening to the news over the radio. He returned to the room and shot Cooper a glance and a nod, knowing what would come later that night but unable to prevent or prepare much for it.

Burnanski arrived last, sullen as ever. The awful smelling cigar he smoked did not hide the smell of alcohol from Cooper. *That's not G.I. beer on his breath,* thought Cooper. *Out drinking heavy stuff somewhere. Supposed to be confined to base. Where has that skunk slunked off to? Not the movies!*

The Andersons

Heavy, wet snow fell in northeastern Illinois. A mailman trudged his way along a tree-lined suburban street. Large elms, devoid of leaves, stretched over the street from either side forming a natural archway of dark, snow-frosted branches. Some residents had shoveled their sidewalks and driveways along the way. Some had not, but the postal worker had tucked his blue-gray U.S.P.S. trousers into tall, watertight black rubber galoshes. He whistled along to himself, remembering Judy Garland singing "Have Yourself a Merry Little Christmas."

The postman crossed the narrow, cinder-strewn roadway and tramped through the snow along the line of houses on the street's northern side, coming now to a small white house with blue shutters. The porch and front sidewalk had been cleared of snow. He climbed four steps, reached into his leather mail satchel, checked through some envelopes. He flipped up the metal lid on the mail slot beside the front door and dropped half a dozen pieces of mail into it. He glanced at the front window as he slogged on to the next house, thinking of the friendly boy, pausing from play or from chores, who had greeted him here in the past. A small banner with a blue star hung in that window. It reminded the postman that the boy had grown and, like so many other young men in the village, had gone away now serving his country.

In the kitchen of that snug little house, Joe Anderson's mother stood by the sink, washing dishes and humming along to some early Christmas music on a Chicago radio station. A small woman with hair more gray than brown, she wore a plain housedress and a faded gingham apron. She saw movement up the driveway, pushed aside a window curtain and caught a glimpse of the intrepid mailman tramping across toward the neighbors' house. She wiped her hands on a dish towel and called to her daughter, "Susan, would you please get the mail?"

"Right here, Mom." A slender teenaged girl came into the kitchen with assorted envelopes in her hand. A junior at the local high school, Susan stood a head taller than her mother. She light brown hair like her older brother and a similar dimpled smile, both inherited from their late father. She leafed through the small stack. "Looks like a couple more bills . . . and something from Joe!"

"Good." Rather than go to the sewing machine where she'd laid her glasses, Mrs. Anderson turned down the radio and sat at the kitchen table, saying, "Open it up and read what he has to say."

Susan sat down opposite her mother at their blue Formica-topped table. Although excited, she took care opening the thin V-mail envelope, trying not to tear the page. V-mail was the primary secure form of correspondence for overseas service members. A soldier would write a brief letter on a single-page V-mail form. The letter would pass through military censors. Technicians copied it in a reduced size onto film and developed it. Transported back to the states, the letter-bearing film would be enlarged. Each letter would be printed onto special paper, which could be folded forming its own envelope. The sealed letter would then be delivered through regular domestic mail. This type of reduced-size correspondence saved vital space and weight on transports from the combat zones. Markings indicated the letter originated from the European Theater of Operations. Her brother's familiar, neat handwriting in small letters filled the margins, squeezing the most onto the restrictions of the single page.

Susan began to read out loud, *"Dear Mom and Susan, We've had a pause in training, so I'm writing a quick letter to you to let you know that I'm safe and well and moving closer to the front.*

The censors won't let us be specific, but I can tell you I'm already posted to one of the parachute infantry regiments and will be joining it soon in the field. I know it'll be tough fitting into a veteran unit, but by God's grace, I've made it through Basic, Jump School and this bit of extra time in England, so I'll trust Him to see me through this new situation too.

"Good boy," Mrs. Anderson whispered.

Susan continued to read, *"Pray for me. I want so much to count for the Lord wherever I'm sent. Pray for the men I'll be serving with that I might shine as a light and be able to win them to the Savior. I expect to meet some tough cases. The Airborne are as tough as they come, from what I've seen and heard, but God can work in their hearts as He has with others in the past. Pray with me that the power of the Gospel will break through to even the hardest heart in my new unit. I want to be victorious in any spiritual battles ahead as well as military ones.*

My love to both of you. I miss you so much, and wish I could be with you for the holidays, but I have great peace knowing I'm where God wants me. Greet the folks at church for me, and other friends and neighbors you might see, and tell everyone I said "thank you" for their prayers as well.

Love, Joe

2 Thess. 3:1a "Finally, brethren, pray for us that the word of the Lord may have free course and be glorified . . . ."

Mrs. Anderson sat still, her moist eyes peering out into space. Her mind and heart toward her son thousands of miles away.

Music from the radio continued playing softly in the background, a choir singing Longfellow's words, written during a time of war and distress almost eighty-one years before: *". . . Then pealed the bells more loud and deep: 'God is not dead, nor doth He sleep; the Wrong shall fail, the Right prevail, with peace on earth, good-will to men.'"*

Mrs. Anderson turned from her reverie and said, "Let's pray for Joe right now." The women reached across the table, held hands and bowed their heads.

* * * * * * *

COOPER

Back in the old French Army camp, just past 1:00 AM, the men had settled into a deep sleep. Reynolds burst into their musty room, threw on the lights, jovially shouting, "Everyone get up 'n saddle up on the double! Jump gear, field packs and light weapons. Assembly outside. Last squad ready has to police the area when they get back."

As Cooper predicted, the night problem had arrived. He had also guessed a main purpose of that night's problem: Shake up the new men by rousing them from slumber and forcing them to orient themselves and move overland in unfamiliar territory.

Men groaned and moaned and rolled out of their bunks. They yanked on their uniforms, jumpsuits, socks and jump boots. They grabbed personal weapons and field packs. Wilcox and Cooper had slept with uniforms on and made everyone have their packs ready, just in case. This move allowed them a few extra moments helping the new men and showing them how to tape up dog tags and jump up and down to detect other rattles, clinks and give-away noises in securing their gear.

This particular night problem presented simple objectives: Simulate assembly following a nighttime parachute drop. Each man would navigate his way across country without compass, wristwatch or flashlight to the assembly point by daybreak. After assembly, the battalion would break into companies and alternate simulated assault and defense of a bridge. Trainers briefly showed them a map of the territory. (*Brief enough to confuse the new guys more than help them*, Cooper thought).

Everyone loaded up in trucks, with the back flaps closed so no one could see where they headed. The entire regiment traveled out into the night on a roundabout route through rural country a few miles outside of the camp. A patchwork of ancient vineyards and family farms divided the Champagne chalk plateau, a terrain more open than the hedgerow-enclosed fields of Normandy's nasty *bocage* country. The vineyards often stretched for hundreds of acres along the southern slopes of hills. The farms had small plots, pastures or orchards surrounded by low fieldstone walls. Pine forest wove between the vineyards and farm sections. Deep stream beds ran along their borders or through the forest land.

The trucks dropped the men off in the darkness along country roads and unpaved farm tracks at intervals of about 150 yards, simulating a scattered drop, and far enough between so that troopers could not immediately see or communicate with the other men along the line. Orders required the men to remain quiet and in place until an aerial flare signaled the start of the exercise shortly before rise of the waxing quarter moon. The signal merely started the operation, with no relation to the assembly areas. The squad's battalion rendezvous would be in an open field beside a large orchard about a mile and a half to three miles west from their drop points.

Cooper, the first of the squad dropped off, paid attention to the wind direction before leaving camp. *Keep the wind on my left, and I'm heading west.*

No stars peeked through the thin overcast covering the sky. The night air felt cold after the confines of the truck. A couple dogs barked in the distance. *Hope things go smooth*, he thought to himself, *but probably won't.*

Some of the old hands, knowing things go easily amiss in parachute operations, especially in exercises with new men, took advantage of the situation. Not waiting for the flare, Vincenti prepared a mound of pine needles in a patch of forest well away from the road and settled down for some more sleep. Friedenfeld, disgusted by the exercise interrupting his night's rest, didn't wait for the flare either. Having a keen sense of direction from childhood and teen years herding cattle out on the high plains and hunting elk around Laramie Peak, he headed for the assembly point without difficulty. He arrived ahead of the battalion and found a spot out of the wind between two trucks parked in the orchard. He leaned back against a pear tree and went back to sleep.

As the night wore on, a stream of other men trickled in. Wilcox and Cooper, dropped off at either ends of the spread-out squad, arrived next after Friedenfeld. An hour after most of the veterans and even some replacements from other squads came in, Reynolds sent Wilcox, Cooper,

Herdlika, Avery and the other non-coms back out to round up stragglers. A half hour later, Vincenti ambled in, found Friedenfeld and went back to sleep as well.

Nurnberg, Tobin and Anderson lost their way early on. Thicker clouds on the eastern horizon veiled the rising moon, blocking that aid in navigation. The trio had cut across country and ran into each other in the confusing maze of a darkened pine forest. The truck dropped Anderson between the other two, and he headed in the right direction, until Tobin, feeling his way along deeper in the forest blackness, discovered the deep course of an unseen creek by falling headlong into it.

"Whoa!" he cried as he took a step into thin air and pitched over into the water: *SPLUNGE!* He panicked and splashed around, sinking under and struggling back up under his heavy pack, not knowing the depth of the water. "Help! Help Somebody! I can't swim!"

Anderson and Nurnberg, hearing the initial splash and Tobin's frantic calls and thrashing about in the water, converged on the sounds from left and right. They stumbled through the undergrowth, dodging tree trunks in the Stygian forest and snagging their clothing on bracken and low branches.

Nurnberg, hurrying toward Tobin's cries, snagged his right boot in some exposed roots. "Oompf!" He tumbled, sliding headfirst down the steep bank into the water not far from Tobin. *SPLASH!*

Vegetation wrapped Nurnberg's ankle, tangling his leg, and he couldn't pull himself out of the stream. Fearful of drowning, he struggled, keeping his head above the water, crying and gurgling in his efforts, "Help, somebody!" *Gurgle!* "I'm tangled!" *Gurgle!* "My head's down in a stream!" *Gurgle! Gurgle!*

Anderson ran to the splashing, gurgling and wailing men. He detected the stream bed before he stumbled into it himself. Holding his carbine above his head, he slid down the dark bank and waded up to his chest in the chilly water. He freed Nurnberg and helped both men up the bank.

"Thanks, Anderson!" said Tobin.

"Yeah, thanks!" said Nurnberg.

"Oh, no!" Tobin said. "Where's my rifle? Maybe I dropped it in the creek!"

"It's only chest deep," Anderson said. "Let's look around for it. I'll help you keep from going under." He dropped his weapon and pack up on the bank.

"All right," Tobin said, setting his own pack beside Anderson's.

Nurnberg took off his pack and joined them.

The trio entered the cold water again and waded around, dragging their boots along the slippery bottom pebbles and feeling with their hands along the muddy banks for something long and heavy. They sloshed around for several minutes until their fingers grew numb in the chilly water and climbed onto the bank again, shivering in the night air.

"G-guess w-we'll have to g-give up," Tobin moaned through his chattering teeth.

Anderson retrieved his weapon and pack and stumbled on something in the dark. "What's this?" Too heavy for a pine branch, he discovered the missing rifle, high and dry, lying on the bank across from where Tobin originally tumbled in.

"Here, sling this over your shoulder," Anderson said. "At least you've got something that's dry."

"Thanks! That's another one I owe you," said Tobin.

"Let's move out!" Nurnberg said, heading off into trees.

In all the commotion, the trio had come out of the stream on the wrong side, and Nurnberg in his impatience began leading them away from the assembly area. Thick clouds on the horizon obscured the moon when they emerged from the forest, so their directional error continued.

"Where's that road?" Nurnberg asked. "Should've come to it by now."

"Hush!" Tobin said. "Listen!"

A distant bell sounded the hour in an unseen French village somewhere far off to their left. The three young men headed toward the sound. They came over a stone wall into a vineyard rising up a low ridge. They continued up the slope along the rows and trellises until they came to a paved road. They began following it.

Anderson raised his hand, halting the others. He crouched down, and the other two did the same. Down low, they could see something moving out of the shadows on their left, silhouetted against the overcast sky.

Nurnberg whispered, "W-what's that?"

Tobin shivering the most in the cold air, said, "A c-cow, may-maybe?"

"I think it's one of the older guys, the veterans," Anderson said. The figure had come out onto the road and walked on ahead of them.

"Th-think we sh-should follow?" Tobin asked in a hushed voice.

"Might as well," Anderson whispered.

"S-safety in numbers," Tobin whispered.

✱ ✱ ✱ ✱ ✱ ✱ ✱

BURNANSKI

Burnanski also didn't wait for the flare. He crept back out to the road after the drop-off truck moved on and headed the opposite direction, having a good guess about his relative location. He came to a crossroads with French road signs and a small shrine—the concrete statue of some French saint mounted on a fieldstone pedestal. By the light of his G.I. lighter, he checked the signs and found himself in familiar surroundings. Burnanski smiled, remembering the little country *taverne*, the French version of a public house. The scene of his illicit drinking hours earlier, located only a half mile north. The small drinking establishment sat beside a *ferme*, or farmhouse, next to a tall windmill pumping water for vineyard irrigation. He ducked behind the shrine and lit a cigarette. He heard the deep *Krump!* of the heavy mortar launching the flare. The signal streaked aloft in a stream of sparks and burst high up above, suspended by a tiny parachute, a single magnesium star descending beneath the canopy of the overcast sky.

Burnanski moved further into the shadows of a hedge, out of the brilliant star shell's thousands of candlepower illumination, and waited for the burning light's slow descent. After it dropped below the far tree line and extinguished, he lit another cigarette and continued waiting out of sight, listening and watching for road traffic.

Coast is clear! Burnanski thought. He stepped out of hiding and headed up toward the crossroads and the quaint little country taverne with its windmill. The faint plinking of an out of tune piano and raucous laughter came to his ear. He thought, *Open for business. Somebody's beaten me here*. That the little drinking establishment opened for business in the middle to the night didn't surprise him. On his earlier visit, the proprietor gave him the impression that—French, German, American—it made no difference to him who slipped out of camp on the sly for a bottle of cognac, hard cider or the famous regional product—Champagne—or what hour they came. As long as they had money, he'd open the bar.

The taverne barely in view, a noise approached from down the way. Two jeeps and a truck came rushing along the intersecting road. Brakes squealed. The vehicles rolled to a stop in front of the country taverne, illuminating it with their headlights.

Get back! Burnanski cautioned himself. Cursing softly, he dropped over a fieldstone wall and crouched in the shadows. He raised his head to eye-level with the top of the wall, watching a squad of M.P.'s pile out of the jeeps and back of the truck. They burst through the taverne door, billy clubs in hand. The door hung open, a yellow rectangle against the gray silhouette of the taverne building. Not much else could be seen, but sounds told of the proceedings: Music stopped in mid-song when the M.P.'s rushed through the doorway. Laughter from within the building died, replaced by loud, argumentative voices. Sounds of blows, furniture breaking, and glass shattering. M.P.'s hustled a half dozen angry, cursing troopers from other companies outside and herded them into the back of the truck. Four large M.P.'s climbed in behind them, pulled up the tailgate and made it secure. A clatter as a pair of M.P.'s dumped an assortment of helmets and other gear from the prisoners into the back of one of the jeeps. Loud protestation in French by the taverne proprietor as the M.P.'s roughly escorted him to the jeep. The engine roar of the jeep and the loaded truck starting up and fading away, back down the side road.

Close call! Burnanski thought to himself. He continued looking up the road to where four armed M.P.'s remained outside the taverne. The M.P.'s split, two by two. One pair waited back inside the taverne. The other started up the remaining jeep and drove it around, out of sight, behind the building. *A trap*, Burnanski thought. *The foxes hoping for more chickens!*

Burnanski climbed back over the wall and started away from the taverne. His combat sense picked up the soft tramp of the replacements' boots on the tarmac and the scuff and swish of their damp uniforms. He paused. The trio of green troops came up to where he stood.

"What are you mutts doin' here?" He demanded.

Recognizing Burnanski, Nurnberg and Tobin kept silence, too frightened to answer.

Anderson spoke up, "We saw you and hoped you'd lead us to the assembly point."

"You all ain't coming with me," Burnanski said. He jabbed his index finger into Anderson's chest. "Especially you, little choir girl!" His hand whipped up, knocking Anderson's helmet backward off his head.

"Just show us the way," Nurnberg said.

"See that building?" Burnanski pointed up the road to the taverne. "There's some guys in there who'll show you!" *Yeah*, Burnanski thought, *they'll show ya right to the stockade!*

Anderson picked up his helmet. The trio moved off toward the taverne, not daring any more questions.

"Thanks!" said Nurnberg over his shoulder.

Burnanski trotted off in the opposite direction without looking to see what happened to the little chicks he sent in to the foxes. An hour later, he approached the assembly point and ran into Cooper.

"Seen Anderson, Nurnberg and Tobin?" Cooper asked.

"Yeah," Burnanski said, "about an hour ago on a road north of here. Some M.P.'s up there. Maybe they helped them on their way."

Yeah, they sure helped those suckers on their way! Burnanski gloated. He strode off to the shadows by the edge of the gathering, sat down, leaned against a tree and lit a cigarette. He chuckled to himself about the fate of the dumb "little chicks," especially Anderson. *Break his poor momma's little heart hearing that her baby Bible-boy got arrested in a bar. Ha!*

CHAPTER FIVE

Rheinland-Pfalz

Early December 1944

Grossholtz

It had been a turbulent summer and autumn for Oberfeldwebel Karl Grossholtz. Turbulent and difficult. As a senior non-commissioned officer in the Heer, or army, he bore responsibility for his company's enlisted men in and out of combat. Changing fortunes of war the past six months had made that difficult work for him, sad work. Naval guns and fighter-bombers blasted His coastal defense regiment from the concrete comfort of their Normandy beach fortifications on D-Day. Allied land forces more than decimated them in the months that followed. His unit regrouped, fought, regrouped and fought, limping in retreat across France back to the defenses of the West Wall. Along the way he had buried many of his men and suffered wounds twice himself.

The rapid collapse of the *Westarmee* during the summer gave him the impression that things might be ending soon. He was ready for it to end, yearned for it to end. Tired of war, he longed for a return to quiet civilian life—desiring no more responsibility than reupholstering furniture in his little repair shop; no more conflict than weekly games of chess; and no more service than the village fire brigade.

The Führer had other plans. The tattered remains of smashed units formed the nuclei of new infantry formations. Planners cobbled together a miscellaneous assortment of *Landsers*—the rough German equivalent of the American soldiers' nickname "G.I.'s"—men gleaned from idle Luftwaffe and Kreigsmarine detachments and wounded returning from hospital, like Grossholtz, forming the new cadre's backbone. The Reich also jumbled new conscripts into the mix, the scrapings from the bottom of the Vaterland's manpower barrel: Old men previously unfit for duty and teenaged schoolboys. They dubbed the new organizations *Volksgrenadier Divisionen*, patriotically combining *Volk,* or "Peoples'," with *Grenadier*, the name of historic, elite troops of the old German Empire.

Grossholtz's mind ran with bitter thoughts. *Rather than admit defeat and cut his losses, the Führer's rebuilding and reorganizing. Something big's coming, something terrible. Heaven help us Landsers live through it.*

The *Volksgrenadiere* obviously fell several quality levels below the superb units that raced across France in the 1940 *Blitzkrieg* and poured into Russia a year later. Their uniforms also showed lower quality, made from synthetic fabrics due to wartime shortages. The new men completed an accelerated training regime. Quartermasters issued them an odd collection of available weapons—from automatic *Maschinenpistole 40's* and captured American semi-automatic M1's to "wonder weapon" *Sturmgewehr 44* assault rifles and single-shot *Panzerfaust* anti-tank rockets. This was another of Führer's inspirations, compensating for lack of training by making the Volksgrenadiers as potent as possible for close-in fighting on the assault. The past week, Grossholtz's regiment moved toward the front in careful, clandestine stages. Each move came at night, from concealment to concealment.

Grossholtz called his men and boys together from the bleak shelter of the leaf-barren cherry orchard where they had bivouacked during the daylight hours. He marched them through the gathering dusk ten kilometers further down to another railroad siding. The night would take them on their last leg, somewhere to the west or north and close to the inescapable fates of war awaiting them.

Grossholtz had guessed the truth. The Führer gathered Wehrmacht reserves according to a plan. Part of the German withdrawal the previous summer concealed the careful pooling of strength for a devastating counter-offensive.

Not all the units contained patchwork infantry like Grossholtz's. Several veteran Wehrmacht infantry and panzer divisions and some from the notorious *Waffen SS* refitted and poised for a stunning blow.

Grossholtz shepherded his platoon to the waiting freight cars. He climbed into one of four assigned to his company, a four-wheeled covered goods wagon, and shined the light of his electric torch around. He saw the interior of the wagon type French military called a *quarente et huit,* a "forty and eight," so named by its capacity for transporting forty men or eight horses. Hooves of livestock or, from the looks of things, artillery draft horses chipped and wore away lower portions of this car's interior walls. No sign of any horses having been transported recently in the car. Musty straw on the floor seemed devoid of any droppings. He climbed into the second car and third cars assigned to his platoon and found more of the same. He inspected the fourth car and turned around to leave when his light chanced upon signs of past human travelers high upon the walls of that car—a chilling record etched there. The old Feldwebel shuddered, took off his helmet. His mouth gaped open. Previous occupants of this particular car scratched messages into the wood. A name and address inscribed here, a short plea to contact a parent or a spouse there. Many names defaced, scratched out, chipped away, but some remained legible. The dates indicated the scratchings originated about three years past. Dutch and Belgian addresses, from what he could tell. The names all appeared to be Jewish. *Jakob, Mozes, Lazare . . . More evidence! The horrible rumors are no mere anti-Reich propaganda,* he thought. *Good thing it's dark for now. However, inquiring young minds will ask questions when the doors are open after daylight.*

He put his helmet back on, climbed down, and split his Landsers and the other non-coms among the cars. The men and boys spread out inside, sitting against the sides or lying down on the straw-covered flooring. Grossholtz sternly reminded his subordinates about prohibiting their charges from smoking, lest a fire break out in the confines of the car. Dirt and dust from the straw could foul firing mechanisms, so he gave orders ensuring proper care for their weapons. He wasn't sure all of his men knew how to clean or even operate them. *Perhaps there will be time to drill that in before we see action,* he thought.

He left an Unterfeldwebel in charge of the older and middle-aged men in each of the other cars and climbed into the remaining carriage, the one bearing the name inscriptions, with the youngest group. The engine's whistle blew. The train jerked and pulled away into the night, gaining speed.

On through the darkness, the rickety cars shook them along toward their unknown destination. They tried to rest. The boxcar was so musty that they kept a door slid halfway open to the cold night air anyway. One of the boy soldiers fitfully sneezed from exposure to the hay. Grossholtz moved him closer to the fresh air, but sat between him and the door opening, lest the lad tumble out in his sleep.

The situation reminded Grossholtz of his Scoutmaster days in the past, leading the village *Pfadfinder,* the pre-Nazi equivalent of Boy Scouts, watching out for his boys. A childless widower, he relished that active responsibility in the years before the Nazi regime disbanded Germany's Pfadfinder organizations, replacing them with the *Hitlerjugend.* Those happier days had been seen him leading village lads on hikes through the forests identifying wildlife, hunting for mushrooms, fishing and swimming in the lakes and sleeping under the stars. *Look where the Hitlerjugend has gotten us,* he thought. *Where are my scouts tonight? Fritz, Hans and Otto dead. Pauli in some stinking Soviet P.O.W. slave-labor camp, if he's still alive. Then there's Gerhard —Poor lad! Dying for acceptance, now a monster of our Führer's making—No! Don't think of Gerhard now. Heaven, help my scouts. Help these other boys and the older men too. Help me keep them alive to return to their homes and families at the end of the war.*

The rhythmic clatter and sway of the nighttime rail journey lulled most of the men and boys to sleep. Four hours and seventeen minutes later that lull met a rude interruption. Rail-cars jolted together. Sleeping men and boys jostled inside. Grossholtz shot out his arm, grabbing the door frame, keeping himself and the near-by lad from plunging out the door.

The train lurched down to a complete halt, wheels squealing and throwing showers of sparks. Grossholtz struggled to his feet, joints stiff from sitting so long. He waved his arms and flexed his legs, brushed off his clothing and leaned out of the doorway, glancing around. Air brakes hissed beneath the cars. A cloud of steam obscured the locomotives up at the front of the train. Dogs barked incessantly in the distance. They were out in the countryside away from any village. A western tributary of the Mosel River gurgled away in the darkness beyond one side of the railroad embankment; a vineyard-covered ridge loomed up on the other.

Grossholtz dropped down to the gravel-covered embankment. He moved away from the train for a better look up and down the rail line. Tracks curved away from view behind. An eerie red-orange glow shimmered on the horizon ahead. Distant, punctuated thundering echoed down the river valley. Flak bursts flashed and boomed high above crisscrossing beams of far-off searchlights. Grossholtz could guess the reason for the delay: British night bombers raiding. A rail yard or factory some kilometers ahead engulfed in flames. Grossholtz thought, *Journeying no further this night, probably.*

The Hauptmann and his young Leutnants came trotting down the beside the train, jackboots scuffing in the gravel fill, banging on each car and shouting orders to load up weapons and packs and get the Landsers off the cars and away from the tracks into cover of the vineyard on the far side of the ridge. Grossholtz knew they didn't want the men stuck inside the train or near it when daylight came. "*Jabos,*" or *Jagdbombers,* the dreaded enemy fighter-bombers with their bombs, strafing cannon and wing-mounted rockets, might catch them here.

The men and boys groaned, cursed and complained about leaving the relative shelter of the old freight-cars, but Grossholtz shooed them off the train and moving up over the ridge. "Tomorrow, we keep under cover," Grossholtz told his men. "Maybe we'll finally learn to field strip these odd weapons while we wait. Tomorrow evening, if the tracks ahead are clear and the train left intact, we will continue our journey."

"Journey to where?" a young voice asked.

"The war's end, I hope."

CHAPTER SIX

Wilcox

Wilcox's earlier observation, about how it would be interesting seeing how Anderson fit in, came to fruition. Almost *too* interesting, as an incident occurred two mornings after the night problem. Even among the generally tolerant troopers of his company, accustomed to eccentrics in and out of combat, having Private Joe Anderson around provided a novel experience. Later that day Wilcox had plenty to write about in his journal:

We picked up three new men and are trying to break them in. We had a night problem soon after their arrival. What a mess after it got started! Even veterans straggled in hours late. M.P.'s arrested a bunch of guys they caught sneaking off to some French country bar. Somehow they rounded up my three new men too, even though the rookies say they only entered the place seeking directions. Evidently, they stumbled into the wrong place at the wrong time. Other troopers had been sneaking off to this place the last couple nights, and the MP's set up a trap. Stockade guards wouldn't release the new guys to the Lieutenant or me. Finally, the Major and the Captain came down and cleared things up.

The next morning we felt pretty worn out. They ordered us out anyway and ran the whole battalion through a harsh physical training session, chastening us for the night problem fiasco! Then they trucked us back out to the bridge site. We alternated assault and defense maneuvers until sunset. The rookies made mistakes all over the place, as expected. Exposing tactical weakness was part of the purpose. We needed to know what we have to work with and help them now before real combat where mistakes end lives.

One of the new men is a bit different. His name is Joe Anderson. He's from

Illinois, outside of Chicago. He'd been attending a college down in Tennessee, studying for the ministry of all things, before he joined up. Nice enough guy, although he seems to pray about everything. Says he even prayed about joining the airborne and about which squad he'd be sent to. (He's the first person I've seen in a long time bow his head and give thanks for SPAM—maybe he'll bring us luck!) His praying didn't get him in good with Burnanski, though. Ski stumbled over him in the dark this morning on the way to the latrine as the kid knelt by his bunk, quietly praying in the wee hours of the morning. Ski's hullabaloo woke most of the barracks.

The other men, new and old, never encountered a barracks situation quite like what happened that morning before reveille: Worn out from the past two days' activity and jolted awake by Burnanski's booming voice to witness a dangerous confrontation.

"Hey, what is this?!" Burnanski snapped. At first, he thought someone was playing an unwise practical joke on him until he saw it was the religious new kid kneeling by his bunk praying. Too much for Burnanski. "Look at this!" he bellowed disgustedly. "Sky-pilot junior's in touch with the Old Man. Momma'd be proud of her little boy."

Friedenfeld rolled over and scolded, "Pipe down!"

Wilcox opened one weary eye. "Lay off, Burnanski! Let the kid pray. We'll all need it if we go back into combat."

Cooper lifted his head and threw in his two cents, "Ski, shut up and let us sleep, huh?"

Burnanski snatched up a sheet of paper and Joe's flashlight from the bunk. "What have we here?"

Anderson said, "It's a prayer list."

"A prayer list, huh?" Burnanski mocked. He held it up and shined the flashlight on it. "Look at this," he sneered and began to read," 'Mom, Susan . . . President Roosevelt . . . General Eisenhower . . . .'" Glancing down the list, the muscles in his neck tensed, and his anger flared, "Hey! What's this? It's the squad! 'Sgt. Wilcox, Cpl. Cooper . . . Pvt. Wendell Burnanski!'"

The flashlight clattered to the floor. The lens shattered, and the light went out. An ugly tension filled the dark room. Cooper sat upright, ready to break in if Burnanski tore into Anderson. Wilcox pulled himself to his feet, also poised to intervene. He'd heard from others about Burnanski like this during the riot in the French city—cold, menacing, deadly!

Burnanski's voice dropped to a whisper, ominous with venom as he ripped the prayer list. "Listen, 'Holy Joe,' I got no time for sissies and no time for God. You keep outta my way, or I'll tear you in two!" He dumped the shreds over Anderson's head. "Pray about that one, preacher-boy!" Burnanski stormed out. The slamming door punctuated his hostility.

Pounding on the wall and muffled yells came from rooms next-door as the adjacent squads protested the commotion and pre-dawn interruption of their rest.

"Need to teach him how to properly close a door," moaned Cooper's voice in the dark.

Anderson retrieved his flashlight from the floor and flicked it on, shaking it back to life. Broken pieces of the cracked lens fell out, but the light still worked. Cooper asked, in the pained tone of one who has risen too early and too abruptly, as he whispered, "Kid, do you always pray early in the morning like this?"

"Whenever I can," Anderson whispered, sorting and smoothing the paper scraps and piecing the list back together. "Usually too busy training the rest of the day."

Cooper lay back on his bunk, shaking his head. "You *are* a 'Holy Joe!' Didn't other guys razz you for it in boot camp and jump school?"

Anderson paused in copying the list onto another sheet of paper. "Sure. Eventually most ignored me," Anderson said, "but a few asked me to pray for their requests too, and a couple guys even joined me from time to time."

"Count me out right now," Cooper groaned, rolling onto his other side. "Still have almost an hour of sleep time left."

Wilcox had never experienced this kind of situation before, but he had been a schoolteacher, so he worked from that. He swallowed his own irritation and faced it with common sense. He rose and stood beside Anderson. He put his hand on Joe's shoulder and whispered, "Joe, holy or not, if you're going on praying every morning, keep it quiet and some place where Burnanski won't trip over you, like the back hallway. There's an old desk there. Nobody's using it at this hour. If anyone who asks about it, tell 'em I gave you permission."

"Thanks," Anderson said. He got up, picked up his fresh prayer list and headed off to the back hallway to continue his prayer time.

Burnanski returned, and the others had gone back to sleep, but Wilcox lay awake pondering the situation within his squad. The combustible mix of Burnanski and Anderson worried him. He rose again and crept out to check on Anderson. He peered down the back hallway and saw by the light of Anderson's flashlight that he knelt in prayer beside the cracked desk chair. Anderson sighed. The flashlight's beam revealed muscles tense in Anderson's face as he focused in prayer.

Wilcox heard Anderson break out in a whisper, murmuring, "Dear Lord, thank you for bringing me to these men. Help me to learn from them and earn their trust. Give me the wisdom to know how to reach them with the gospel. Guys call me "Holy Joe." They mean it as a joke but help me live up that name. Help me to be holy so that You might fill me with Your power. Grant victory in the battle for these souls, especially for the soul of the man named Burnanski. Help me to somehow show him the love of Christ."

Having this "Holy Joe" Anderson in my squad is going to be very interesting indeed! Wilcox thought.

CHAPTER SEVEN

Südeifel

Greier

The rugged countryside rippled with ridges and ravines, blanketed with thick pine forest—a sparsely populated region of scattered towns and villages and few paved roads or rail lines. In winter, it seemed impassable. For some, these features made it a quiet backwater away from the main conflict consuming Western Europe; for others, these same features presented an avenue of strategic opportunity. SS-Sturmbannführer Gerhard Greier strode from his log headquarters bunker into the twilight. He scanned the darkening skies and noted the increasing clouds. He smiled and thought, *A wonderful sign!*

Greier switched on his pocket lamp, directing its hooded beam over the bulk of his *Befelspanzer*, or command tank, a *Panther*, hidden beneath the camouflage netting stretched over it by his crew. He noted to himself, *Order Schaefer to have the white paint I requisitioned for the hulls mixed and ready in case these clouds bring snow before the counterattack.*

The Panther was fresh off an assembly line in the Ruhr. He'd abandoned his previous armored command vehicle, a massive *Tiger*, back in France. A temporary bridge could not bear its 54 tons when his shattered unit staggered in retreat out of the Falaise Pocket in August. He missed the Tiger's overwhelming firepower and thicker armor, but better now using this medium tank because of terrain and road constraints expected during the coming offensive. *Besides,* he mused, *even a medium Panther proved more than a match for any of the Amerikaner armor.*

He'd led his surviving men back to the *Vaterland* in early September for rest, reorganization and refitting. Because of aggressive defense, gallantry and leadership in rear guard actions battling allied armored forces in Normandy (one of the last *Tigers* out of Falaise), his idol, the Führer himself, awarded him Oak Leaves for his *Ritterkreuz*. Hitler promoted Greier to a new command, this *SS-Sturmbataillon*, an assault battalion of *Panzergrenadiere*, or armored infantry, bolstered by a battery of nine brand new *Sturmgeschütz IV* armored assault guns, a type of turretless tank. Basking in self-glory, Greier drilled his men relentlessly from mid-September to early November in preparation for the coming counteroffensive. Now they lurked under cover, fierce predators soon to pounce in horrendous fury upon unsuspecting foes of the Reich.

He adjusted the medallion at his throat, inhaled and blew out a puff of thick smoke from one of his last Amerikaner cigars. *Excellent things! Soon I shall obtain more of these*, he thought, and addressed his tank commander, "Raise the netting more over this turret, Kurt, and let it sag. Must look like random foliage from the air. Don't give them any suggestion of an outline."

Heels snapped together. "Jahwol, Mein Herr!"

The Sturmbataillon cut *Feldlagers* deep in the forests off the main highway. Russian P.O.W. laborers prepared these parking bays, removing specific trees without leaving obvious holes in the overhead forest canopy. Camouflage netting enhanced the concealment. Deceptively narrow access trails led through the trees. The slave laborers pounded the trails firm and scattered with soil and pine straw, concealing tread marks, oil leaks and other signs of the presence of large armored vehicles.

Orders forbade telltale smoke from fires and restricted outside activity by day. Greier's disciplined men kept out of sight in log bunkers and beneath the camouflage canopies until dark. Daytime vehicular traffic required special written orders. Allied reconnaissance aircraft flying overhead had no hint that his nine "SturG IV's," many half-tracks and other vehicles crouched beneath the trees below.

Detached from main SS units farther north, the Sturmbataillon would lead an assault in the vanguard of the southern thrust, blasting through the enemy lines, bolstering one of the Volksgrenadier Divisions. *I shall lead them to triumph*, he pledged to himself. *Even old men and little boys cannot help but be victorious in my wake.*

"Pass the word, start engines at sundown. Routine check. Let them idle until warm enough to check fluids."

And this crack unit itself won't be idle long, he thought. *A week, a fortnight maybe? No, the New Moon approaches! Only a favorable downturn in the weather, sufficient cloud cover, and we're unleashed! Everything is according to plan, the Führer's own brilliant plan, not from those idiot, defeatist generals in OKW. Frightened old women, trust the Führer! Dismiss all doubt from your thoughts. He'll lead us to victory yet. He shall defeat these decadent stooges of Bolshevism and Jewish international finance. He has willed it. Victory and glory for the Reich! Victory and glory for Gerhard Greier! Shattering our foes like Thor's legendary hammer. We shall turn the tide of this war and purge the shame of retreat with Amerikaner blood! We'll drive these invaders from the soil of United Europe. How satisfying that'll be!*

He strutted down through the trees to the highway. Headlights masked, a convoy of *Panzerwerfer*, half-track-mounted rocket launchers, rolled along under the deepening cover of approaching darkness, even more deadly firepower heading to forward positions.

Yes, how satisfying that'll be. Certainly, Crossed Swords will hang beneath the Oak Leaves on my Ritterkreuz when this operation is over.

CHAPTER EIGHT

The Lieutenant

Powerful forces clashed along the line. Probing thrusts sought out weaknesses and exploited them. Men fell beneath their foes only to rise again, ignoring mud and sweat, pressing onward. The football coaches demanded an effort and élan on the practice field equaling that of the division's operations on the battlefield.

An ancient cattle pasture before the war, the long, oval-shaped patch of open land measured over five acres, tree-lined and level. Conquering Germans appropriated and butchered the grazing beef for their kitchens and commandeered the enclosed pasture as a vehicle park for confiscated local automobiles, trucks and tractors. Liberating Americans returned remaining vehicles and took a different interest in the property. They rented the flat open space from its rightful owners for use as football practice fields. Division headquarters arranged the formation of two football teams to begin regular practice on the former pastureland, duty permitting. The schedule of practice would culminate in the hand-picked teams playing against each other in a touch football game on the parade ground for the entertainment of the entire division on Christmas Day.

Team rosters quickly filled, using former college and semi-pro athletes from the various regiments. Coaches choose many of these players from the division's surviving veterans. The original cadre's men possessed outstanding physical ability, strength and endurance. They endured and excelled through intense training in the States, England and subsequent combat in Normandy and the Netherlands. These veterans drove new troopers, coming in later, to rise to the original standard.

Lesser talent made up a couple auxiliary or "taxi" football squads, giving the primary football teams adequate practice and providing a pool of back-up players. The Lieutenant, having football experience at The Citadel, recruited and coached one of the taxi teams.

Combat simulations and field problems continued each day and sometimes during the nights, but football practice now replaced most of the physical training schedule for those on the ball teams. Determined to make his taxi squad the best, the Lieutenant pushed them hard. (Competitive by nature, he harbored a desire to beat one of the official teams in a scrimmage, a prospect rapidly dimming as coaches of the official teams began raiding his roster to replace injured players on their squads.) During one of these scrimmages another incident between Burnanski and Anderson occurred.

The Lieutenant drafted anyone in the battalion with significant football experience not already on one of the official teams. He brought Cooper in as a team manager and assistant to the coach because of insight gained working pro and college football games at the Polo Grounds. Wilcox bowed out of play because of his sore back and became unofficial assistant to Cooper, but four members of his squad became involved as players. Although he preferred baseball, Tobin had seen some playing time on defense and as a back-up quarterback in high school. Nurnberg played second team as a two-way back at his Milwaukee County school. Anderson made varsity as an end his senior year at his west suburban school. Burnanski, the best of the bunch, earned five bucks extra a week while playing on a rough-and-tumble industrial league team for his steel mill. One of the official teams elevated him onto their squad, replacing an injured player, after observing Burnanski's brutal ferocity during scrimmages.

Northern France had little American football equipment available. The YMCA flew over a dozen footballs from bases in England and whatever other equipment they could scrape together. The rest was make-do: Jump boots instead of cleats, battered tanker's helmets discarded by an armored division, and second-hand rugby jerseys courtesy of friends back in England.

The Lieutenant ran his team through some basic drills and plays. He demanded intensity, even in two-handed touch football. What he saw pleased him. Tobin threw accurate passes most of the time. Nurnberg, though small, showed some agile moves as a halfback. Anderson had good hands.

A couple days later, the Lieutenant's team played their first full practice game against one of the official teams. Most of the company came out, supporting their Lieutenant and his team. The taxi squad struggled against the opposing team's first-string players. They fell behind early on but began holding their own against their opponent's second string later in the half.

If we can't win the game, at least win a quarter, the Lieutenant thought. Just before the halftime break, he called for a time-out. "We need a score to finish this half," he said. "We're running a reverse. Haven't tried one yet."

"Haven't practiced one either, sir," said Tobin.

"They won't expect it, then—the element of surprise," the Lieutenant said. "Surely y'all ran some type of reverse at your school."

"We did," Tobin said. "Hand-off to the halfback, who fakes a run to the right and pitches to the end, who is running around left."

"I'm game," said Nurnberg.

"Me too" said Anderson.

"That's the spirit!" the Lieutenant said. "All right, men, that's our play: Look left, hand-off and fake right, pitch and run left. Nurnberg and Anderson, hold onto that ball when it comes your way!"

The players returned to the field. Anderson took position right of the line, Nurnberg as halfback took position behind Tobin. Tobin took the snap from center; hesitated a beat, looking left. Defenders reacted to his glance anticipating a pass. He pivoted, handing off to Nurnberg, who sped off right, following the fullback. Defenders shifted the opposite direction to stop his run. Nurnberg pitched the ball off to Anderson running by the other way. Tobin's feint caught the defense by surprise. They swarmed after Nurnberg, baffled by the rapid changes in direction.

Anderson dashed left around his line and turned up field. Only one defender possessed a chance of stopping Anderson from charging all the way to the end zone: Burnanski. Veteran of the cagey style of the mill-worker teams, Burnanski kept his eyes on the ball. He caught the changes in direction and flew across the defensive backfield. He brushed aside the left end's feeble block. He slammed into the fleeting Anderson three paces from the end zone, a shoulder knocking the wind out of him. The referee blew his whistle ending the play and the half. Anderson lay sprawled on the field, gasping for breath. Primal Burnanski harassed his fallen prey, cussing insults.

"Nice . . . hit!" Anderson wheezed up at the beast towering over him.

A couple other defenders grabbed Burnanski by the arms and tugged him away. Cooper ran over and lifted Anderson's arms above his head, helping him breathe easier until he could regain his feet and stagger off to the bench.

The Lieutenant jogged onto the field, intercepted Burnanski and said, "Let's talk."

Everyone else trotted off to either bench and turned to see what would happen next. The Lieutenant and Burnanski stood out on the field alone—Burnanski, feet wide, chest out in contempt; and the Lieutenant, feet also wide, leaning into Burnanski's personal space.

"You sent those kids into the arms of the M.P.'s during that night problem," The Lieutenant said in a low voice, knowing the others were watching. "Heard about you tripping over Anderson the other morning and threatening him. I saw you cut him down today. You know it's supposed to be 'two hands below the waist,' yet you took him to the ground. Intensity, not brutality!"

Burnanski snorted, "Said himself, 'nice hit.'"

"It was, but you didn't stop there with it, you went on, standing there cussin' at him. Remember who your opponent is—and I'm talking about this war, not football."

The Lieutenant walked away, leaving Burnanski alone, and thought to himself, *Burnanski situation's not working out. He has to go or he'll hinder the platoon, weaken the whole company. Time to talk to the Captain and the Major about shipping him out! Even before the Christmas game if I can!*

Horns honking, two jeeps and a staff car raced along the highway. The vehicles turned onto the field. A one-star general's pennant adorned the olive drab automobile's hood. The Lieutenant and other officer coaches and referees trotted toward the vehicles. Reynolds jumped out and met them as they approached. At first, players thought the acting division commander and some other brass had merely stopped by, observing progress with the teams, but Reynolds shouted, "Officer's call!"

The Lieutenant and the other junior officers climbed into the vehicles, which hurried off, leaving Reynolds behind, running out onto the field and calling players and spectator soldiers together. Moments later, everyone double-timed it back to the barracks leaving footballs, helmets and water buckets behind.

Bigger struggle than a football scrimmage now, the Lieutenant thought as the jeep drove him through the base. *Major says the Burnanski issue's on hold, every unit goes as is, including Burnanski's. Maybe combat's the outlet he needs anyway.*

* * * * * * *

As Christmas Time 1944, approached, the quick victories of summer and early autumn gave many people the impression that the conflict in Europe might end soon. After all, Paris had been liberated without massive destruction. Allies possessed most of France, Belgium, Luxembourg and part of the Netherlands. Thwarted at sea, battered from the air, and sent reeling back on land from east, south and west, Nazi Germany seemed ready to crumble. Back in the States, the Training Command began diverting new troops, originally earmarked for the European Theater, to the Pacific.

Just as Allied hopes grew, when peace in 1944 seemed within reach, Adolph Hitler unleashed the hidden might of the Wehrmacht in a sudden counteroffensive through the heavily forested Ardennes region of Belgium. Allied commanders thought this rugged area, with limited roads and narrow lines of communication, unsuitable for large-scale military operations. Where only five enemy divisions appeared to be operating, twenty-five heavily armed German divisions ripped into the thin American lines.

U-boats lurking far out in the Atlantic detected the approaching weather system Hitler's gamble depended on and radioed advance data to Berlin. On Hitler's order, OKW had set the operation into motion. In the moonless, pre-dawn hours of December 16, 1944, heavy German artillery, rocket and mortar fire pulverized unwary American defenses. As that terrible day unfolded, armored spearheads crushed defenders, wreaked havoc in rear areas, and raced on west. Heavy overcast and fog neutralized Allied air support. Communications broke down. Pandemonium and panic spread along the American front. Nine teams of German infiltrators, fluent in American English, dressed in American uniforms and driving captured American vehicles, spread confusion and sabotage behind the lines.

U.S. Army units, many without combat experience, crumbled in the face of the onslaught. Some surrendered *en masse*. Others fled in dazed chaos. Here and there, valiant men held their ground though surrounded, fighting in the bitterest of struggles with little hope.

German victors marched most captured Americans off to P.O.W. camps, but Hitler gave his *Waffen SS* secret orders: *Be swift and brutal; let nothing slow the advance; kill prisoners if necessary.* Near the tiny hamlet of Wereth, Belgium, an SS reconnaissance patrol beat, stabbed and shot eleven G.I.'s from a veteran African-American unit. Outside the near-by town of Malmedy, *Sturmtruppen* mercilessly gunned down over eighty other captured

G.I.'s herded together in a snowy field.

Hitler's last big gamble—winning the war by splitting the Allies in the west—became the greatest and bloodiest pitched battle ever fought by American land forces. It dwarfed even Desert Storm by comparison. Only the total of both sides during the Battle of Gettysburg exceeded the number of American casualties.

The Wehrmacht OKW, high command in the west, named their operation *Wacht am Rhein*, "Watch on the Rhine," deceiving Allied intelligence into thinking their troop movements merely strengthened defenses along the Rhine River. Official U.S. Army historians would dub it "The Ardennes Counteroffensive." The common G.I.'s gave it a simpler name. They sized up the maps, noted the bulging German westward advance penetrating American lines, and called it "The Battle of the Bulge."

CHAPTER NINE

Eastern Belgium

December 18, 1944

Wilcox

Wilcox's journal entry early that morning:

I hope you'll be able to read this. I'm writing scrunched up in the back of a truck. Something's up. A day ago, I stood with a bunch of the guys watching football practice when some brass drove up, stopped everything, and ordered us to pack things up on the double. Later, word came over the radio of a German counterattack up in Belgium. Looks like the war-weary Airborne's high-tailing it up to hold the line. That's our reward for doing the tough jobs: We always get the next tough assignment!

They're sending us into this just as we are, not up to full cadre, and without essential equipment repaired or replaced. My squad only has eight instead of twelve. Airborne platoons heading into combat usually have two lieutenants, a leader and a spare as an assistant, but ours didn't receive a spare before we trucked out. Sgt. Reynolds will have to double as the unofficial assistant. Maybe it's better that way, having his experience and wisdom rather than somebody right out of O.C.S. with no combat sense.

We grabbed what weapons we had, but we're short on our heavier stuff, like mortars, machine guns and bazookas. Maybe we'll be refitted wherever we're headed.

Things had been so quiet up until now that some stateside conference called our division commander and his assistant back to Washington. Our soft-spoken division artillery commander, left minding the store, didn't hesitate in getting things rolling. He had us roused before dawn, packed up and loaded like cattle into these heavy cargo trailers—no benches and no springs! At least this particular trailer has a canvas roof. Some don't, and it's been snowing off and on as we head north. So much for Christmas in Paris!

Watching from the back of the truck, we've passed through the historic city of Sedan, scene of two French defeats by the Germans in 1870 and 1940. Hope the city doesn't fall again while it's in American hands. We've crossed the Meuse River and seem to be heading north and east through the Walloon region of Belgium. We're moving roughly parallel to the border with Luxemburg. Our destination is unknown, at least on the squad level. The region has picturesque countryside, kind of a rolling piedmont area like we have east of the Blue Ridge Mountains back home, with wooded ridges, ravines and river valleys. Quaint villages with their ancient churches, little industrial towns, small farming hamlets—all glimpsed in a flurry of passage without a chance to know their names or history.

A great big hurry getting us to the fight. We have top priority. M.P.'s clear all other traffic off the roads while we rush through. When we headed out before dawn, these tractor-trailers ran with their lights on full, no black out slits. If they continue driving this way after sundown, I hope no German planes come looking for a target.

The convoy of tractor-trailers streamed on deeper into Belgium. Civilians paused along narrow village streets, and farmers glanced up from fieldwork as the long, noisy caravan sped through the urban and rural communities on the way. By the volume and speed of the traffic, they could guess that something serious loomed up to the northeast. The haste of the caravan cast a doubtful shadow on their recent liberation. In cafes and markets, homes and workshops, Belgians debated growing speculation that this development meant battle retuning to their doorsteps or worse.

Most of the airborne troopers rode in stake-sided tractor-trailer rigs, useful for hauling freight but offering nothing beyond the windbreak of their canvas covers and some straw strewn over the wooden floor for passenger comfort inside. Within the confines of Wilcox's trailer, several squads tried to make the best of it inside their jostling transport. Some of the men tried to sleep, resting against their packs. Some sat and talked. Others rolled dice and passed the time gambling in a cleared area up in the trailer's nose. Wilcox sat at the rear with Anderson, Cooper and others in the fresher air and better light. Here they could also glimpse the passing countryside.

Cooper rubbed itchy eyes. He kept on sneezing. "Have to sit back here. Dust from this straw drives my nose crazy."

Anderson reached into his jumpsuit and handed Cooper a fresh handkerchief. "Keep it," he said. "My Aunt Betty just sent me a dozen of them. She's sweet, but getting on in years, and her memory isn't too good. She forgot she'd sent me another dozen a couple months ago, so I pass them on. They're monogrammed. Think of the "A" standing for 'Airborne' instead of 'Anderson.'"

Cooper blew his nose loudly. "Ahh, that's better. Thank Aunt Betty for me," he said before blowing his nose again.

Anderson peered over at Wilcox, twisting his head, trying to see what he'd written. "What's that you're always writing about?" Anderson asked.

"It's his 'war diary,'" Cooper said, pointing at the notebook between sneezes.

"I'm keeping a journal of my all experiences, like riding in this extremely comfortable cargo trailer," Wilcox said. "It's the historian in me. I like a firsthand account. In this case, I write my own."

"A regular 'Ernie Pyle,'" Cooper added. "Careful what you say, he's recording it for posterior-osity."

"The word's 'posterity,'" Wilcox said.

"Aaaaah, same difference!" laughed Cooper.

"What'll you do with your journal?" Anderson asked.

"Don't know yet. Perhaps I'll write a book when it's all over," Wilcox said. "At least I'll have it to share with my folks and remember observations and experiences . . . if I make it through."

"Yeah, Big 'IF!'" Cooper sneezed on the last word.

Wilcox showed Anderson his last few pages. He pretended to check some of his gear while Anderson quietly read through what he had written so far that day. Wilcox stole a glance at the serious and thoughtful expression on his face.

"This is good," Joe said as he carefully handed the notebook back. "Straightforward, accurate and unembellished, unlike some of the newspapers. When I first arrived, I told you a bit about myself, why I joined up, but what about you? Why'd you join the army and get into the airborne?"

"When the president and congress declared war, I was the middle my second year teaching history and geography to junior and senior high students," Wilcox said.

"Surrounded by dames," shot Cooper, "but chose to be surrounded by the likes of us!"

Wilcox glared mildly at Cooper for his interruption. "Hardly any of those young ladies would go by the description "dame," and all of them: A) Too young; and B) Too lofty for a guy like me. I was more of a sloppy younger copy of 'Mr. Chips,' *sans moustache*, than a Cary Grant to my students. Now, where was I in my explanation?"

"About to tell me why you entered this war," Anderson said.

"Honestly, I thought this might be the big story of my lifetime. I had no wife and kids holding me back, so when the school year ended, I signed up."

"And like you asked me, why the airborne?"

"He's too honest to be a supply clerk and too good a cook to work in the mess," Cooper shot in.

"Seriously," Anderson asked, keeping the conversation on track again, "why'd you volunteer?"

"Well, I didn't exactly pray about it like you did," Wilcox said. "But I did give it some deep thought when I was going through basic and infantry school. My Grandpa Wilcox volunteered during the Spanish-American War, but Congress hadn't appropriated money for sufficient troop transport, so his unit only got as far as Tampa. My Dad, much more of a scholar than I am, spent his World War I tour at the War Department in Washington, DC, analyzing intercepted cables. Although I can't complain because he met and married my mom at that time—she worked as a civilian clerk. I didn't want to be left out of this one. I wanted to experience war from up front. When the airborne came around seeking volunteers, I signed up. I guessed that the paratroops would be in the thick of it. I hit that nail on the head! I kept in good physical shape before coming in, always hunting and hiking around in the Alleghenies and playing the college baseball you've heard about. Still, Camp Toccoa's jump school was no picnic, but I made it."

"You have a degree. Did you consider O. C. S.?" Joe asked.

"I could've become an officer," Wilcox explained, braiding a couple long pieces of hay together, "but I didn't want that kind of responsibility. Back then, didn't even want them to make me a corporal. I figured I may kill my share of Krauts, but I didn't want to cause another G.I.'s death though some careless decision I might make. I'd read enough about Shiloh, Chancellorsville and Gettysburg to understand that."

"Yeah," Cooper added, pointing with his toothpick for emphasis, "other people's stupid decisions have a nasty way of gettin' guys killed in a permanent sorta way."

"I only wanted to be responsible for myself," Wilcox concluded. "But war doesn't give exclusive options like that. Even if you're not in official authority, you have to look out for others in your unit too. Eventually, I let them make me a sergeant so at least I'd have more of a say in looking out for my own squad."

Anderson turned toward Cooper. "How about you?"

Cooper scratched his jaw stubble and took out his toothpick. "Nobody's asked me that for a long time." His face assumed a rare thoughtful expression. Something about Anderson's sincerity made him drop his wisecracking facade. "Everyone was steamed up over Pearl Harbor and what was happening in Europe. Brooklyn's full of immigrant families, so most folks had relatives sufferin' under Hitler's thumb or Mussolini's. I knew I needed to go and fight—and I mean *fight*. Don't like to do things halfway. Didn't want to be stuck stateside or in some rear echelon. I figured the paratroopers would do their job on the front line or beyond, so I pulled every string I could to get in. How about you? I guess your family's really proud of you."

"Don't have much family myself," Joe said. He took out a small photo, an even younger-looking version of himself in uniform flanked by his mom and sister, taken after basic training. "Just my mom and kid sister at home, a couple aunts and uncles. My dad is with the Lord."

"Nice family," Wilcox said. Familiar with teenaged female pulchritude, he handed the photo back adding, "Cute sister."

"Thanks."

Cooper cocked his head, not ogling the image of Joe's pretty sister, but puzzling at his last statement. "What do you mean, your dad's 'with the Lord?'"

"A car hit and killed him about nine years ago," Joe answered.

"That's too bad," Wilcox said.

"Yeah," said Cooper.

"God is good. Dad accepted Christ as his Savior a couple months before the accident. He worked as a milkman," Joe explained, "and people used to put gospel tracts in the empties. He'd pick them up and read them. What he read bothered him a lot, but God used that in calling him to Himself. Dad finally put his faith in Christ. He didn't know only weeks later a drunk driver would hit him as he stepped away from his truck making an early morning delivery."

"That's tough," Cooper said.

"I'm thankful he turned to the Lord before it happened," Joe said. "Life is short. Folks never know when they'll face eternity."

"Right now I'd just like to know what we'll be facing in the next few days," Wilcox said. "Ought to arrive sometime tomorrow, at this rate, or we'll drive right on into Germany."

Burnanski staggered back from the front of the lurching trailer, keeping his balance by holding onto the metal ribs holding up the flapping canvas roof. "Any of you guys lend me some dough? I'm figurin' on making a come-back."

"I'm broke," Wilcox said.

"How 'bout it, Coop?" he asked.

"You still owe me from the last time," Cooper said, jerking his toothpick out for emphasis. Burnanski continued looking at him, knowing he held something back. Cooper stuck the toothpick back in, reached into his top pocket and yanked out some Provisional Franc Notes. "No greenbacks, but here's some francs if you want 'em, but you'd still better pay me back!"

Burnanski glanced down at Joe Anderson with disgust. "I won't bother asking the sky-pilot. Probably start preachin' me a sermon on the evils of gambling."

Joe gazed up him with his unique sincerity. "Rather than merely condemn sin," he said, "I'd prefer showing you how you can be saved from it."

Others had cursed Burnanski before, and he'd been goaded by haughty insults, but this unaccustomed calm talk by Anderson all the time infuriated him more. His eyes narrowed; his face turning red; and veins in his neck bulging from pent up rage. "Fat chance of that," he spat. "Your God is outta my life as far as I'm concerned. Better pray up, kid—you'll see what hell's like where we're goin'."

"I will pray, and I'll pray for you too," Joe said.

Burnanski reached down, grabbing Anderson by his field jacket, lifting him from the trailer floor until their faces almost touched. "I told you before: Don't waste your prayers on me! I hate your God, and I hate your guts! If the Krauts don't kill you after we get there, I just might do it myself!"

Joe Anderson never flinched, but faced him squarely and said simply, "I'll still pray."

Burnanski's knuckles turned white. Wilcox and Cooper could see his rage boiling. They began rising to their feet to hold him back, but he abruptly shoved Joe Anderson back against the side of the truck. He leaned down, spoke barely above a whisper, "I mean what I say!" and staggered back to the front of the trailer.

Wilcox, Cooper and several on-lookers at the rear of the trailer sat for a moment, stunned to silence by the outburst and close call. Joe Anderson's eyes followed Burnanski as he moved away. Wilcox whistled softly, letting off tension.

Cooper leaned over toward Joe. Pointed with his toothpick and said, "I'd keep clear of him if I were you, kid. As you've seen, Burnanski's poison when he's riled."

Wilcox said, "Sometime when he's not around, ask me to tell you why I think Burnanski's this way." He reached over, straightened out Joe's collar and began to laugh. "You amaze me. I've seen men with real guts in battle, but you won't back down from Burnanski and have a confidence that's strange to me. Where do you get this?"

"Like to know myself," Cooper added.

Joe Anderson regarded both of them for a moment and said, "Would you let me show you some verses from the Bible?"

"Go ahead," Wilcox said. "I'm tired of talking football, politics, and the war. At least it'll be a change of pace."

"We got nothin' else to do," Cooper added, "and we're short on chaplains."

As the dice continued rolling in the front of the truck, Wilcox and Cooper huddled with Anderson and his small Bible in the back. Nurnberg, Tobin and a couple of others listened in, as well. Anything to break the boredom. Theology never interested them much before, but, then again, they'd never met someone with a spiritual sincerity like Joe Anderson either.

"I've seen you reading from that little leather book. I had one of those little New Testaments once,' Cooper said, looking over. "You know, the khaki-covered ones the Y.M.C.A. gives out to G.I.'s. Lost it stateside. Didn't know they made a whole Bible that small."

"Might stop a spent bullet if you carried that in your pocket," Wilcox said. "Read about that happening more than once in the Civil War."

"My mom visited a bookstore in downtown Chicago and found a Bible I could carry with me anywhere," Joe said. "The pages are small and so is the type." He paused, looking around at them all. "Let me first ask you all a question, which will lead into what I want to show you."

"Ask ahead," Wilcox said.

"A big question: If you died today, where would you spend Eternity?" Joe asked, his directness and sincerity disarming. He took his religion seriously, and that made them carefully consider their answers.

"Heaven, I guess," Wilcox said. He thought, *At least I think that's the answer. All these past years of church and Sunday school must be pointing me that way.*

"That's what I'm shootin' for," added Cooper.

"What does each of you base that on?" Joe continued.

Cooper thought for a moment, and so did Wilcox. Anderson touched on something neither had been called on to explain before. Cooper answered first, which gave Wilcox and the others another moment to think on the question.

"Well, for me," Cooper said, "I was baptized in my church when I was a baby. Suppose that's good for something."

"I've always thought God would weigh my good works against my bad works," Wilcox said, "and somehow I'd come out ahead." *That seems a pretty fair answer*, he thought to himself. *Many people think that way.*

Joe listened to their answers and said, "Let me give you some things to consider. First, about baptism, do you think Hitler's going to heaven?"

Cooper snorted with disgust, followed by a sneeze, "That dirty little paperhanger's gonna split Hell wide open!"

"It's a documented fact that his parents had him baptized as an infant," Joe said.

"What?" Cooper blurted in disbelief.

"And about good works," Joe continued. "Is there anything you've done that's greater than the work of Christ on the cross?"

"What do you mean?" Wilcox asked.

Joe opened his Bible and thumbed a few pages over until he found a verse from Ephesians, turning the little volume so Wilcox could see the words on the small page while he quoted them from memory. "The Bible says here in the Book of Ephesians, chapter two, verses eight and nine, *For by grace ye are saved through faith, and that not of yourselves, it is the gift of God, and not of works lest any man should boast.'* You see here that salvation is a gift from God based on faith in the work of Jesus Christ. There isn't a work of my own I can do to match that, and no ritual can take its place. The Bible also says in both the Old and New Testaments that *"The just shall live by faith."* Here is where my confidence lies: My faith in Jesus Christ and His power to save."

"I was baptized as a baby just like Cooper," he continued. "I attended Sunday school and went through confirmation, but when I was sixteen, I came to realize that, although I'd been a part in these things, my personal faith hadn't been involved, and none of these equaled Christ's sacrifice of Himself on the cross. I needed to put my faith and trust in Jesus Christ alone. As the Apostle Paul told the Philippian Jailer, "Believe on the Lord Jesus Christ and thou shalt be saved." I prayed and asked Him to forgive my sins and save me. From that day to this, I've known for sure I'm on my way to heaven because it's Jesus who made it possible."

He concluded, "Keep in mind that the Bible also says, 'There is a way that seemeth right unto a man, but the end thereof are the ways of death.' Don't let any person or any human idea fool you into thinking you have anything short of God's plan for salvation. I've been baptized; I've tried to live a moral life; and I've trusted Christ as my Savior. Which of these three has saved me from my sins?"

Cooper's forehead wrinkled. "Never looked at things that way before," he said.

"Well . . . rich food for thought," Wilcox said, not knowing exactly what else to say.

They talked on through the morning. Joe Anderson and what he showed them from the Bible were different from anyone and anything they had come across before or during the war. Tobin asked Joe to explain who the Philippian Jailer was, which led to Joe retelling the account of Paul's conversion and missionary journeys from the Book of Acts. Wilcox added some insights into First Century culture from his own study of the Roman

Empire. Everything Joe shared meshed right in with that.

All day long, the heavy trucks ground their way northward. Nearer and nearer to the front, increasing traffic from retreating units heading the other way began to clog the road, slowing down the progress of the northbound trucks.

Wilcox's journal entry later that afternoon:

Still in the trucks. Spent most of the daylight hours talking with Joe Anderson and a handful of others, a regular impromptu symposium about religion and early Church History. He really knows his stuff.

In mid-December, nightfall comes early in Northwest Europe—keeping in mind that we're nearly as far north in latitude as Newfoundland, and the calendar's approaching the "shortest day" of the year. We're all tired now and trying to catch some shut-eye while we're still under shelter, if this flimsy canvas cover counts for one. We've closed the back flaps now. Not much to see after sundown. Even before dark, it began growing cold, and I hope it doesn't get much colder. None of us has any true winter gear. I haven't been issued a heavy overcoat yet. I'm wearing a sweater under my field jacket and the faded jumpsuit I wore in Holland over my new uniform. Reynolds warned us it'll be colder where we're headed. We did the best we could, putting on two or three pairs of socks, an extra pair of pants and whatever else we might scrape together before leaving the camp. Our trucker says Ike's been sending all the gas and ammo he can to the front, leaving overcoats, galoshes and gloves piled up at the coast, gambling that the war will end before we need the winter gear. Wish the dear general rode in this icebox with us right now.

* * * * * * *

Greier

The SS-Sturmbataillion continued its inexorable advance down the snowy road. Heavy overcast shielded their rapid progress from Allied aircraft above. Fog and snowbound forest ridges screened their movement along the road below—until too late for the unsuspecting, feeble defenders they had encountered so far.

Like a knife through Butterkäse! Greier mused to himself. *Like the early days in Polen and Frankreich—so ridiculously easy!* "Die Herrenrasse auf dem Marsch noch einmal!" he said aloud, savoring the sound of the old slogan—"*the Master Race on the march once more!*"

So far, he'd caught Amerikaner units off guard. His tanks and men crushed their futile resistance or over-ran those in retreat. He turned his vehicles and his attention toward a small hamlet straddling the road up ahead. Pushing on through, he sought to capture the next major town and its road network beyond, then secure crossings over the River Meuse. Other SS Panzer units to the north had been designated the honor of capturing Antwerp, one of Europe's greatest ports. *I'll show them! As we did in Frankreich, I will turn this battle into a race to the sea,* the Sturmbannführer thought. *First the village, then the town and road network, a bridgehead. After that? On to the Nordsee!*

BOOM! A flash of white and orange interrupted his meditations as one of his lead half-tracks took a hit above its left front wheel from an American 57mm anti-tank round. The heavy vehicle wobbled off toward the shoulder of the road, out of the column. Panzergrenadiere jumped out. They deployed behind cover the disabled vehicle offered, returning fire on the anti-tank gun situated behind some overturned farm carts and timbers stacked between the hamlet's nearside buildings. Machine guns mounted on the half-track and others behind it fired on the American position. Green tracers converged on the anti-tank gun, marking the spot for the command tank.

Ach so! Greier chuckled to himself, *Some fools stand and fight.* He dropped down into the turret and closed the hatch. "Road-block on the right, where tracers converge, range 150 meters. High explosive. Fire as we clear the disabled vehicle," he directed. His tank's turret traversed right as it crawled around the injured half-track.

BOOM! Another anti-tank round, this one glancing harmlessly off the tank's thick front armor. The tank's turret finished traversing in the direction of the enemy roadblock. The muzzle of its 75mm main gun lowered for close range.

"Feuer!" The main gun fired. The high explosive round's glowing tracer streaked on target. Obliteration! Pieces of carts, timbers, gun and gun crew tumbled through the air as the roadblock disappeared. Survivors fled back through the village.

"Abandon that half-track! Other vehicles shove it off the road and resume advance!" Greier shouted into his microphone. *This the best they can muster against me? Swat the fly and drive on!*

CHAPTER TEN

On the Road to Belgium

In a desperate attempt to stem the flood of the advancing Panzers, General Eisenhower rushed his only available infantry reserves, the XVIII Airborne Corps--two weary, depleted airborne divisions--directly into the storm of battle. Hundreds of heavy tractor-trailer rigs of the famed "Red Ball Express" dropped their regular loads, picked up the men and sped them to the front. One airborne division, the 82nd, hurried to Werbomont, Belgium. There it blocked the crucial advance of the I SS-Panzer Corps, buying time for American units taking defensive positions on the northern shoulder of the Bulge near St. Vith. The other division, the 101st, rushed to reinforce units of the 9th and 10th Armored Divisions hindering the southern German thrust near an old Belgian market town named Bastogne.

* * * * * * *

Wilcox

The big trucks growled on northeast into the Ardennes as far as they dared. Artillery flashed, thundered and rumbled, an approaching storm east and north. The anxious truckers dropped the division's men over a mile and a half southwest of the town. They swung their rigs around for loading personnel and wounded evacuating south, eager to leave danger behind them.

MP's stood guard outside a church.

"Drop your packs inside," the Lieutenant ordered, an ominous sign of looming combat. "Hopefully, we'll retrieve them later," he told his men as they filed through. "Can't be burdened with 'em now."

"Grab extra socks and a change of underwear, just in case," Reynolds advised each squad. "Leave bed rolls and the rest."

Wilcox and his men tramped behind the Lieutenant through Bastogne's narrow cobblestone streets. Equally narrow brick and stone townhouses and shops with their sharply peaked roofs flanked the streets. The ancient buildings stood shoulder to shoulder, some overhanging the roadway below.

The airborne troopers passed ragged columns of regular infantry trudging the opposite way. Civilian residents peered from windows and doorways. The townspeople eyed the opposing streams of soldiers with a mix of apprehension and apathy—fearing the return of harsh overlords and resigned to the relentless ebb and flow of conquerors and liberators, a European fact of life going back to the Celts and Romans.

The retreating infantry were a mixed lot. Hardened veterans in battle-stained uniforms moved along with discipline and determination. They headed back to regroup and fight again. Others, dissolved into mobs more than any military formations, shuffled and straggled toward the rear. Some of these haggard men shouted, "The Krauts will kill you!"

The troopers filed by many wounded men, their field dressings stained by blood. They passed others shaken, confused, staring with vacant eyes. Many men had lost their equipment and weapons. Others abandoned theirs upon seeing the troopers, glad to be out of the fight.

"What do you think, kid?" Cooper asked Anderson, witnessing this sad spectacle.

"Reminds me of something from the Old Testament Book of Job," Joe said.

"Yeah," Wilcox said. "These guys have been through a grinder!"

"And we're headin' right into it! Cooper observed.

"Firemen to the rescue," Vincenti said, "Running into a burning building when everyone else is running out!"

Reynolds came down the line, ordering, "Grab what you can from those retreating. We're short on ammo and other supplies."

The troopers slung bandoliers over their shoulders, gathered extra grenades and stuffed rifle clips into their cargo pockets until they bulged. Cooper kept his eyes peeled for other useful items, collecting a hatchet, pick ax and a couple full-sized shovels. "I know these come in handy," he said.

"Haven't been this loaded down since Normandy," Wilcox said. "At the time, I thought it too much. Proved to be barely enough when the real fighting started."

They came upon a retreating weapons squad ditching their .30 Cal. machine gun and other weapons before boarding a truck.

"We'll take those!" said Reynolds, rushing in. "Wilcox, bring your squad over!" Second squad grumbled a bit about the extra load, but Reynolds' no-nonsense glare kept them from being too vocal in their protest. Burnanski shouldered the machine gun. Nurnberg took up the tripod. Vincenti and Friedenfeld carried a bazooka and some ammo for it. Cooper and Tobin toted machine gun ammo boxes and spare barrels. Anderson grabbed an abandoned B.A.R. with its bipod, ammo clips and a couple extra barrels.

Wilcox's battalion hiked through the town's outlying eastern district. On the far side, they split up by companies, fanning out on roads and a rail line leading into hilly, forested terrain broken by pastures and small farms. Without commands being given, veterans in Wilcox's company spread out into combat intervals in columns of two as they approached the front lines. Scouts hurried on ahead, and flankers split off and moved out into the trees on either side, as the company marched out east along the railroad tracks. This unspoken and automatic movement impressed upon the new men that they'd truly entered a combat zone. They followed the experienced men's example, checked their weapons and remained alert.

Their company turned north. They hiked along a narrow road through a large pine forest. The trees grew evenly spaced and of a uniform size and showed signs of cultivation. Long branches spread out high up on the trunks, forming a canopy of sorts above the thick growth of scrub plants and briars covering the forest floor.

"Reminds me of a tree farm back home," Nurnberg said.

"Or pulpwood for some mill," said Tobin.

"These forests supplied a lot of charcoal to the Belgian steel industry once," said Wilcox. "Read about this area in the last war and the beginning of this one. Krauts attacked through here in 1914 and 1940."

"Looks like they're pulling the same trick a third time," Friedenfeld said.

The sights and sounds of near-by battle grew and grew—almost continuous flashes and explosions in the distance, lightning and thunder from a violent storm of deadly combat.

"Some heavy fightin' thataway," Cooper said from experience.

"Hope we're winning," Vincenti said.

"Win or lose, hope it doesn't come our way before we have a chance to dig in good and deep somewhere," Friedenfeld said.

The company emerged onto a snow-covered tarmac road, continuing northward for about three-fourths of a mile. The dark forest continued along slopes of ridges on their left, broken by farmland on their right. Dawn approached under an overcast sky. Patches of fog obscured the open countryside and left everything damp and dripping. Senses tuned to the distant battle tried to determine if it shifted closer or drifted away.

The company split up by platoons as they came along the road. The Lieutenant led his own squads on past one of the other platoons already digging foxholes in the forest. He halted his men further down while the rest of the company streamed on north. The forest thinned out at this spot as it sloped down from a long ridge to a low stone wall on the western side of the road. A pasture or farmer's field opened up beyond a wire fence on the eastern side, but in the fog made determining how large or small the field extended difficult. A narrow, "two-rut" gravel lane ran along the southern edge of the field and intersected the main road at an angle. More forest bordered either side of the field. The northern side of the field sloped down sharply to a creek. It flowed from the ridge, through culverts under the road, into a deepening ravine between the field and forest on the east side.

The Lieutenant checked his hand-drawn map and called his squad leaders together. Using a stick, he sketched a diagram in the mud beside the road. He drew a line representing the previous front. "On the big scale, here's where the lines were the other day. Germany here, Belgium and Luxembourg here and here, France down there. Krauts broke out, poured in from the east, over-running or pushing back everything between here and the Siegfried Line." He drew a circle with lines radiating from it, a seven-legged spider. "On the local scale, here's Bastogne and it's roads. The Germans must capture it to continue west, and we're setting up here to block 'em. The enemy has tanks, half-tracks, artillery, and several divisions of fresh troops. We have what we carry in with us plus a few units who haven't retreated yet, but they're low on supplies too. We hold here at all costs. The Krauts must not take Bastogne!"

The Lieutenant paused, letting his last comment soak in. He pointed to the ridge west of the road. "On the small scale, we're establishing the company M.L.R. up slope, north-south, stretched out along this ridge-line and the next one north." He rubbed out the drawing and began a new one. "Our position's overlooking this road and the farms beyond to the east." He drew a line representing the road and three long ovals, like sausages, along one side, one "sausage for each of the company's platoons. He pointed his stick to the middle oval. "Here's the road and the company's platoons. We're the middle, facing east across the road. 1st platoon's to the south, on our right, back the way we came, and 2nd platoon's north, here on our left, beyond this creek. Company command post and heavy weapons situated behind them."

He drew a thinner line representing the creek and extended the line representing the road. "The country road here runs follows the base of the ridge, roughly north and south along our front. It curves west about a mile south, and intersects a two-lane road after it crosses those rail tracks we were on." He drew lines showing the tracks and the main road and continued drawing as he talked. "North of here, our road runs on for half a mile and hits another main road from the east. Major roadblocks with anti-tank guns are being set up at both intersections, north and south. Our company's heavy weapons are up north in support of the one that way. Our job down along here is keeping the Krauts from slipping through the farmland in between and flanking either roadblock. They can't run tanks through the forests, so we must deny them control of the roads." He paused and glanced briefly at each of his squad leaders. Wilcox and others nodded their understanding of his operational description so far. "Nearest aid station is being set up on the reverse slope of the next ridge behind us, about 500 yards southwest. That'll also be our first fall-back position and rallying point. Battalion HQ is south of that, at a small rail station west of the roadblock. Whatever ammo, food and other supplies we might receive will come out from there. We'll use runners for communication until we get some field telephones set up. If things get too hot, shoot up a red flare, everyone else come running in support. If we capture any prisoners, MP's will receive them at the aid station and take them on to HQ."

The Lieutenant drew five smaller ovals within the platoon's long oval, representing his rifle and heavy weapons squads. "Wilcox's squad will anchor the platoon's left, with our flank on this creek. Deserted farm buildings are supposed to be across this field, about 200 yards north of here in the fog. The creek here runs down into a wooded ravine east of this field and the buildings. The ravine deepens as it runs off to the northeast. That farm lane curves along the south edge of the field toward the farmhouse and sheds. Wilcox, establish an O.P. at the base of the ridge here. Keep an eye out for Krauts coming either way on the road, the lane, across the field or along the creek. The Krauts may push armor through the farm here."

The sounds of distant fighting rose to a new intensity. "By the sound of it," the Lieutenant said, "some of our boys still holding up the Krauts in a village east of here, but they could pull back at any time. Supposed to fall back south of us, but y'all watch out for 'em over this way just in case. And use the current sign "Yellow" and countersign "Hammer" with everyone—I mean *everyone*—even if they're wearing a jumpsuit with a 'Screaming Eagle' patch. Rumor has it that the Krauts have guys running around dressed up in American uniforms. Don't trust anyone just 'cause they seem to be G.I.'s or know the name of Orphan Annie's dog!"

The Lieutenant paused, looking around from face to face, gauging reaction, before continuing. "This stretch of road is closed to vehicles. Unless H.Q. tells us otherwise, assume any traffic along here is hostile.

"Wilcox, 2nd platoon's picking up some mines at the north roadblock and bringing them down this way. Send two men up with the guys from Herdlika's squad n' fetch your share. Lay out yours at this intersection. After that, send a couple men down the lane to scout out that farm. I need to know the layout and if it's truly deserted. Don't want a trigger-happy rookie firing on some poor farmer or any livestock they hear moving around in the fog. Any questions?"

"What about air support?" Wilcox asked.

The Lieutenant gazed up at the sky. "None so far. Don't count on any 'til things clear again. If our flyboys ever show up, use red smoke or panels to mark your positions."

"If we're facing armor, do we have any more bazooka ammo? Only came up with a few rounds for the extra tube we picked up."

"I'll try to scrounge up some more and send 'em over if we got 'em. I'm stretching the rest of the platoon on back down to the next company south. We have two more farms to watch. My command post and the platoon's mortars will be between you and third squad on your right. After we dig in, we'll take turns running regular patrols between the stretched out squads. Don't want any Krauts infiltrating between us. Again, remember the sign and countersign. Check back with y'all later. Carry on!"

"Yes, sir!" Wilcox said.

"The rest of you follow me!" Having seen the terrain firsthand and establishing his platoon's left flank, the Lieutenant led his remaining squads to their positions back to the south.

Wilcox's eye twitched as he relayed and elaborated on the Lieutenant's instructions. "Friedenfeld, Vincenti, Nurnberg and Tobin. Leave the bazooka here. Take one of the machine guns and start digging us in under the trees along the military crest of this ridge. Clear fields of fire under the forest canopy down to the road along here where it intersects this lane. Burnanski and Cooper, hike on up the road with these guys from Herdlika's squad and gather whatever mines 2nd platoon has for us. Bring 'em back and lay them out obstructing this road at the mouth of the lane. Then probe up the lane and scope out that farm, see if anyone's there. Watch for civilians and for stragglers retreating from the firefight east of here. Be wary of the stragglers—you heard the Lieutenant's warning about Krauts in G.I. uniforms. Leave me the other machine gun, a shovel and that pick ax. Holy Joe and I'll set up an observation post over there by the wall. You remember the sign and countersign?"

"Yeah," Cooper said. "Sign is 'Yellow,' and 'Hammer' is the counter."

"Don't forget to use 'em in case some jumpy new guy in the 2nd Platoon thinks you're Krauts in disguise," Wilcox cautioned. He turned toward Anderson and gestured for him to follow. "Welcome to the war, kid." They lugged the machine gun, tripod and tools over to the side of the road. Others came by and deposited ammo cases and the bazooka beside them before heading over the stone wall and up the ridge.

"You dig first while I start keeping watch," Wilcox said. "We're too close to the sounds of that fighting for us both to be digging. Besides, I want to see your foxhole technique."

Anderson grabbed a shovel and started to scratch the leaves and pine needles away from the ground, clearing a place to dig beside Wilcox next to the roadway.

"No, other side of the wall. Over there looks pretty good," Wilcox directed, pointing the folded tripod at a spot beneath two large trees about twenty yards away. "Among the trees and behind this wall's protection. We can move stones around to make us a firing platform. We'll be sheltered, not obvious and still have a clear view of the field and roads, especially that farm lane. Would've reviewed stuff like that back in England if they hadn't been in such a hurry packing up."

Anderson moved over to the indicated spot, picking a gap between two large trees. The forest ran in an irregular border along the edge of the road. Some leafless bushes and weed stalks along the front of the wall might help screen them at ground level. The road had a slight curve at this point because of the creek. If the fog lifted, those in the observation post would be able to see down the road for almost a hundred yards in either direction, up the lane and across the field off to the north toward the farm buildings. They would cover the lane at an angle, exposing anything approaching along it to a broader field of fire.

Wilcox brought the machine gun, tripod, and ammo cases over to the two trees while Joe began breaking up the top ground layer with the pickaxe. Wilcox brought the bazooka over, as well. He moved some stones from the wall for a temporary firing position and set up the machine gun tripod behind it. After mounting the gun, he leaned against one of the two trees near Anderson, resting his aching back while peering out and listening into the fog.

After a while, Joe paused in his digging, shuddered and smiled. "I guess I'm a bit jittery right now."

"Take a deep breath, calm down and keep your head," Wilcox cautioned. "This is for real. Any slip-up could be our last. No kidding when they say, 'the Krauts play for keeps.' Shoot to kill or you'll be killed. Nervous soldiers tend to fire high. Keep your bursts low, down at the waist. That way if you shoot a bit high, you'll still hit something." He stiffened at a noise, dropped behind the wall and swung the machine gun toward the left. Anderson crawled beside him and took up the ammo belt feeding the machine gun. Out of the dark came the sound of boots scuffing on the road. "Halt!" Wilcox called.

Cooper answered, "Yellow!"

"Hammer!" Wilcox shouted back. "Advance!"

Cooper materialized emerged from the fog with Burnanski, the two men from Herdlika's squad and four other troopers. "We got the mines," Cooper said. "They'd already moved them down our way as far as Sgt. Avery's position. Neighborly folks up that a-ways. Lent us guys to help carry 'em and said there's another set of mines laid out north of here at an intersection with a firebreak and trail halfway between here and the big road north."

"Good to know," said Wilcox, "if fighting brings us up that way. I'll report it to the Lieutenant"

Herdlika's men and two of the helpers continued on south with their mines. The other two helpers set down their loads and returned up the road, back to Avery's squad. Cooper, laden down with mines, headed over to the intersection between the road and the lane.

Burnanski set own his load of mines down at the lane, came back and grabbed the pickaxe and the other shovel. He paused by the wall, sneering down at Anderson on the other side, "Hey, Holy Joe, hope you were prayin' about that fox hole before you started diggin'—maybe that'll be your grave!"

"Thanks for the reminder," Anderson said, not looking up as he kept on digging. Burnanski stepped closer, trying to gauge Anderson's reaction, whether to push him further or leave him alone.

Cooper trotted over and took the pickaxe from Burnanski. "Move along, Ski. Pick on the kid later."

Burnanski spat into the foxhole at Anderson's feet and moved on.

Cooper and Burnanski scraped away trampled snow from the tarmac in selected spots. They utilized the pickaxe in breaking through the crust of the road and the packed gravel of the lane. They laid out the rectangular mines in two alternating rows at the mouth of the lane and across the main road just north of the intersection. They dug additional holes at random around the mines and filled them back in, disguising the pattern. The mines themselves consisted of rectangular, olive drab metal cans, rounded on the ends like cans of Spam, but flatter and broader on two of the sides, weighing less than five pounds. The charge within contained enough plastic explosive to kill or maim a man or disable the treads of a tank or half-track. A large, hinged pressure plate located one of the can's flat sides triggered the mine. An olive drab cloth bag slipped over the mine, keeping the pressure plate free from stones or other debris interfering with the triggering mechanism. The men filled in loose pavement chunks, gravel and dirt around the mines without any further concealment and removed the retaining pins, setting the mines. An unwary armored vehicle might lose a track hitting a mine, giving the bazooka team a chance to finish it off. A damaged vehicle might also block other approaching vehicles, forcing them to slow or halt, avoiding other mines or dummy holes, while exposing themselves to fire from the rest of the squad and the platoon's mortars. Without air support, the best Wilcox and his men could hope for was holding the enemy up long enough for reinforcing platoons from north and south converging on their position and driving off the remaining enemy. That was the defensive theory, at least, based on the terrain and what their stretched out company had to work with.

Satisfied with their work, the men from Avery's squad headed back. Cooper returned the shovel and pickaxe to Wilcox, and joined Burnanski.

The pair faded into the fog, scouting down the lane toward the distant farm buildings.

Wilcox paused, listening to the forest around him. The muffled sounds of men preparing their foxholes under the trees up slope reached his ears. The distant firefight boomed, thundered and threatened. Near at hand, Joe Anderson puffed and grunted as he excavated the moist Belgian sub-soil. The growing foxhole gave off a damp, earthy smell. Pine roots protruded around the sides.

Joe struggled with another tree root for a few moments. After he twisted it off and yanked it out, he glanced up at Wilcox and said, "Been meaning to ask you about Burnanski, as you suggested. What's the story behind him? Why's he so angry and bitter?" He picked up his shovel again and continued digging.

Wilcox peered out into the fog toward where Burnanski had gone, making sure he'd moved well out of earshot. "It's a long story," he said, "so I'll try to give you the 'Reader's Digest' version. Burnanski's been one of the best troopers in the regiment, maybe the whole division, from what I've seen. He was an acting platoon sergeant but got into a big mess the weekend before you arrived. They busted him all the way back to private. Even before that, he'd teetered on the edge of trouble when not in combat."

"Heard a little about that."

Wilcox shifted his weight and paused for a moment, listening first to the forest nearby and then to the distant rumble of combat. Satisfied with what he heard for the moment, he continued his explanation, keeping his voice low, "Burnanski's prone to drinking and loves to gamble, but I think those are just surface signs of inner trouble. One tough kid before he joined up. These tough cases often become that way because they hurt on the inside."

"I can believe it," Joe said, "with Burnanski at least."

Wilcox bent down, opening the breech and adjusting the belt for the machine gun. "Burnanski's been alone most of his life. Has no real family—this regiment's probably the closest thing to one he's known," Wilcox took out the belt, worked the action on the gun a few times and fed the belt back into the gun. "He's as smart as any of us college guys, but dropped out of high school and worked in a steel mill to survive. Then the war came."

Wilcox paused again, listening. Far-off sounds of the firefight had diminished. "Steel-working's a defense-related industry, so Burnanski could've stayed out of all this if he wanted, but for some reason he joined up anyway. Not for the pay; not for the adventure. Patriotism may be in it, deep down somewhere, but it's my theory he sought an opportunity to belong to something important, a cut above, and to be accepted, appreciated by and depended upon by others."

"Yeah, everybody needs that. Everybody needs friends," Joe said.

"Well, he finally found some here in the airborne. One of them became a close buddy, a guy named Ed Gluszcak. They met in jump school and became sergeants in the same company when it formed up. Think Burnanski's strong and tough? Gluszcak was stronger and tougher, if you can believe it. Guy's called the duo 'The Polish Mob.' In the Normandy drop, transports panicked, scattering us all over. Fighting in small isolated groups, Gluszcak and Burnanski saved each other's necks, and those of many other guys, for that matter. With less than a platoon of other troopers and no officers, they accomplished their company's D-Day objectives."

Wilcox stopped again. The rumbling in the distance had become sporadic. "Then came Holland. You may've heard talk about a narrow road corridor connecting and supplying all the British and American airborne forces along the salient leading to Arnhem. 'Hell's Highway," we called it. They assigned us the job of keeping part of it open. Many Krauts fled when we first jumped into the area, but came infiltrating back in, gaining strength, giving us fits."

"Had your hands full?"

"I'll say! Constantly out on patrol, watching for attempts to cut off our road or re-take villages strung along the way. Like most of Holland, it was flat country. Small thickets, wood lots, and clusters of farm buildings scattered around, but a lot of open land. A high water table too. Dikes, canals and ditches running all over the place to drain it. The Dutch build their roads on raised land above the fields or along the top of dikes. Their villages stand out, like islands on high ground, above all the low countryside."

"I've seen some pictures," Joe said. "Newspapers over in England carried a lot of reports about it, though mostly about the British forces."

"Well, Burnanski served with Gluszcak in another battalion at the time," Wilcox said. "I'd heard plenty of stories about what happened there and more details when they talked with me about Burnanski coming into this squad." Wilcox examined the hole Joe was digging. "Make it a bit longer over this way, gives some room for the bazooka team beside the machine gun crew, in case something big and nasty comes crawling out at us."

"Okay," Joe said. He took up the pickaxe and began breaking through the tough surface at the new portion. "Heard Burnanski was up for some medal at one time."

"He was. Deserved it too."

"Well, what did happen?"

"Krauts retook a small Dutch village—only a dozen houses, a few shops and a small church."

"And cut off that main road, right?"

"Yeah, they ambush the next supply convoy coming along, destroying some vehicles and pinning truckers down in ditches just outside of town. Burnanski's platoon comes running to their rescue. The Krauts lie in wait. Burnanski's platoon comes under heavy mortar and machine gun fire out in the open. His platoon leader can't withdraw and leave the truckers to slaughter or capture, and he can't stay put and get his men pulverized."

"So he attacks, right?"

"Now you're thinking airborne!" Wilcox said. "He splits up his men, coming at the village from both ends. Burnanski and a squad are sent crawling along a ditch, attacking from the south; the platoon leader will charge in with the remaining squads from the north. As they get in position, Gluszcak, their company first sergeant, shows up with another squad and rallies some of the truckers to provide covering fire."

Wilcox paused again. The sporadic battle noise to the east had died down to irregular blasts, like the last scattered kernels of giant popcorn in a gargantuan pot.

Wilcox continued, "On signal, Burnanski's platoon attacks. At first things go well. The charge from both ends of town confuses the Krauts, but they recover. Their machine guns up on the church's roof turn on the charging troopers. Kraut mortar fire shifts onto them as well. Men are cut down short of cover, including the platoon leader. Burnanski brings his remaining men through, street by street, on the south end. Gluszcak takes command of the north element and fights through the streets as well. Another surprise in the town: The Krauts are supported by two tanks, one on either end of the central square, blocking traffic through town.

Gluszcak's group suffers heavy casualties but knocks out a tank and advances to the church. Burnanski himself damages the remaining tank's turret, jamming it. The disabled tank withdraws from the village. Gluszcak, wounded by now, crawls his way up to the church's roof and silences the gun crews. Burnanski joins him up there and helps him turn the guns on the retreating Krauts. Things seem in hand when an artillery barrage rains down on the village. When it lifts, men hurry up to the church roof and find Burnanski, wounded and unconscious, shielded beneath Gluszcak's dead body. Troopers clear the town's streets and buildings, taking over 30 prisoners, and the convoy continues on. Gluszcak is nominated for the CMH, posthumously. Burnanski is up for the DSC."

"Then what happens with Burnanski?" Joe asked. "Heard of a bar fight."

"The press picks up the story about Gluszcak and Burnanski. First in *The Stars and Stripes* over here and then the papers back home. At the end of November, the two airborne divisions are withdrawn from the line and sent to separate camps in Northern France. The first weekend, troopers from both divisions head off on leave to the same French city. A big mistake. No one's been on leave for over two months. Everyone has a lot of steam to blow off. Fights break out all over between the rival divisions and grow into a riot. Burnanski has a part in it, but witnesses say he's sitting in a bar, minding his own business, when some cocky guys from the other division provoke him. They'd read about him in the newspapers and begin taunting him, starting with the old joke that the eagle on our division patch is 'screaming for help.' When that bad move gets no reaction, they push further with mocking insinuations about Gluszcak and Burnanski's heroism. The fools should've left Gluszcak's name out of it. Burnanski snaps and goes berserk on them with bare fists and bar furniture. M.P.'s bust up the brawl. Burnanski's hauled off to the stockade, but his taunters are hurried off to the hospital.

"As bad as that?"

"As bad as that. Broken ribs, busted jaws and more. Something has to be done about Burnanski, short of a formal court martial, but kept out of the press. Burnanski's quietly busted down to private, and his medal recommendation is withdrawn. Sending him elsewhere might blow the story open, so he's shuffled within the division and lands in our squad. A second chance, at least 'til things blow over.

"That doesn't seem to be working out," Joe said.

"Yeah, I'm afraid not," Wilcox said. "But we get rushed up here, plugging the line, so all that's on hold for now."

The distant crash of battle had stopped. Intermittent rumbles sounded from farther away. Near at hand, only the sound of Anderson's shovel, the voices of the men digging in up the ridge and the drip of moisture from the trees broke the forest's silence.

"Even before we left Holland, Burnanski had changed. Guys who know him say he's jumpy now whenever he hears Kraut machine gun fire, probably reminding him of that day. He's brooding on it a lot. He acts as tough as ever, but he's wounded inside. I think he's angry with himself for not saving Gluszcak. Angry with God too, for taking his best friend. That's why a "Holy Joe" like you irritates him so much."

"God is his enemy. Makes me his enemy too."

"'Fraid so."

Anderson and Wilcox switched positions. Between shovel loads, Wilcox continued his discourse. "It's hard for any new man to fit in, find acceptance with the veterans. Being in a unit like this—training, drilling, facing violent death together—bonds men together like no situation in the civilian world. I guess you'd say we have a kind of love for each other, a brotherly love. We understand each other, trust each other, risk our lives for each other if it comes to that. I think that's the real strength in our army—not superior weapons or strategy, but the ties of brotherhood between the fighting men in each squad, tank or gun crew."

Anderson nodded. "Jesus said, 'Greater love hath no man than this: That a man lay down his life for his friends.'"

"That's what I'm talking about," Wilcox said. "We've got guys here who've gone AWOL from hospitals and stole their way back to this unit rather than be sent as replacements to some other division and guys they don't know and trust. New arrivals like you are outsiders to that, like unwanted stepbrothers. It's not your fault, but the veterans resent you for taking a departed buddy's place. Burnanski's a hard case where you're concerned. If you can prove to him your worth as a soldier, that you have the sacrificial kind of love you just quoted, then maybe he'll begin to open up and accept you."

"I begin to understand him a little bit, and my place in it all," Anderson said. He stood up and walked a short distance toward the road, listening and watching, trying to make sense out of the fog and out of the story he had just heard.

"I think you've handled yourself well," Wilcox said. "Keep a low profile if you can, but don't cower before Burnanski. That'd be worse than standing your ground. Strength and courage will earn his respect if anything will."

Time dragged on. Wilcox and Anderson finished up the hole and kept watch.

"I'm getting concerned," Wilcox said. "Cooper and Burnanski are taking longer on patrol than I thought."

Joe heard a sound coming from the east. "Somebody's coming."

Wilcox swiveled the machine gun toward the lane. Joe squatted beside him and straightened out the ammo belt feeding it.

"Halt and be recognized!" Wilcox shouted.

A voice called out of the fog, "Yellow!"

Wilcox answered, "Hammer! That you, Coop?"

"May not look like General Taylor, but I know Orphan Annie's dog's named 'Sandy!'

"'Leapin' Lizards!" Wilcox said. "'Bout time you showed up. Almost sent a patrol out looking for my patrol."

"Got delayed pickin' up some friends," Cooper called. "Meet Poppa, Momma, big sis' and little bro'." Four civilians, a Belgian man and woman in their thirties, a slender girl about twelve years old and a skinny boy about eight emerged with Cooper out of the fog. He escorted them around the mines and led them to the observation post. The man and woman, relieved to see more Americans, carried some bundles of clothing. The two children stared wide-eyed at the new troopers Wilcox and Anderson. Cooper jerked his head back toward the fog. "And there's more."

Two beard-stubbled and bedraggled G.I.'s walked out of the fog and came wide around the mines, carrying another man on a makeshift litter between them, his legs wrapped in bandages. Burnanski brought up the rear.

"Found this family hiding in the farm cellar with these engineers," Cooper said.

"Sgt. Foley and Privates Hartford and Pace," said the engineer non-com carrying the front of the litter. "We ran a sawmill and supply dump north and east of here, cuttin' lumber for winter quarters. Orders came to blow up supplies and the mill and pull out. Everything almost primed and ready when Kraut recon units raced in on us and shot up our vehicles. We scattered for the woods. Some didn't make it." He nodded down at the man lying on the stretcher. "That's when Pace here took two slugs. The others moved on west, but Hartford and I volunteered to stay behind with him. We carried him as far as Monsieur Solvay's farm over yonder. They hid us in the cellar the last two days."

At the sound of his name, Monsieur Solvay spoke in rapid French, "Nous pouvions entendre les combats dans le village est d'ici et je savais ce que quelqu'un sur ce chemin dans le brouillard, mais il avait peur que plus d'Allemands. Nous craignions des représailles pour aider les Américains."

Cooper glanced at Sgt. Foley, who shrugged, "I don't speak much of the language."

Wilcox spoke up. "Well, I can make out enough to know he's saying they heard fighting east of here. They knew somebody was also over this way in the fog, but feared more Germans and reprisal for aiding G.I.'s."

"Yeah, are we ever glad to see you guys!" Hartford said.

"What's the situation down that way?" Wilcox asked.

"Farm's all clear now," Burnanski said. "A two-story stone house, barn and a couple small out buildings. Lots of pigeons but no livestock."

"Krauts seized cattle and horses in the area last summer before they pulled out," Foley said.

"The lane continues on through the farm about another quarter mile," Burnanski continued. "Runs along another couple fields, past an orchard, and comes out on a north-south, two lane road. Took a look-see down that way, while these folks made up a stretcher and packed up. No traffic, but the fightin' over east of here has stopped. Could hear tanks or half-tracks far off in the fog, east and south. Not ours by the sound of 'em."

"Burnanski, lead the family and the engineers over to the aid station," Wilcox said. "The medics can take a look at Pace and move the family along into town. Coop, you go down the line and fetch the Lieutenant over there too. He'll want to hear your report, the engineers' story and any other info these Belgians have to offer. Tell him about the mines you heard about north of here."

"Will do!" Cooper said. "One thing before we go." He reached into his jacket and pulled out a couple sticks of gum. "Here you go kids! Some real American chewing gum for keepin' quiet on the way over."

"Merci," whispered the boy.

"Merci beaucoup!" said the girl, with a slight curtsey.

Cooper grinned. "That's my name in French—'Beau Coop!"

* * * * * * *

GROSSHOLTZ

The boys riding in the captured truck laughed as if on an outing. Their apprehension about combat had given way to a giddy euphoria. They had merely yelled, fired a few weapons around and the Amerikaner had run before them like rabbits.

It's been too easy, Grossholtz thought while sitting at the rear. *A false sense of victory. Our foes will turn and bite us if we don't watch out.* The old Oberfeldwebel warned his men and boys, "These troops fleeing before us are as green as we are. Once a man starts running away in battle, it's hard to get him to turn again and fight. Don't get the wrong idea. More determined foes, fiercer battles are ahead."

The elder men, less buoyant, more concerned about their immediate future, took his words to heart, but many of the young ones scoffed, a foolish optimism born of Nazi racial superiority propaganda and distorted by their limited combat experience.

The truck slowed, nearing the outskirts of another hamlet, their next objective. They would support the Panzer assault here. The old non-com's eyes, two sober beacons, gazed out at his men from beneath bushy, salt and pepper gray eyebrows. His stare, combined with the increasing sounds of the battle they approached—explosions accented by machine gun fire—quieted the revelry of the younger soldiers more than his words.

Good. They're taking it more serious now. He thought. *May save their lives this next time.*

The truck slowed more. The noise of battle increased.

"Check your weapons," Grossholtz said. *Sounds like we'll need every one of them.*

* * * * * * *

In the rugged, heavily forested Ardennes region, the Wehrmacht and SS Panzer divisions with their tanks, half-tracks, and other heavy equipment depended on the few roads for mobility. A valiant defense, patched together from surviving American forces and newly arrived reinforcements, thwarted the Germans' intended main thrust again and again in the northern part of the Bulge around Stavelot and St. Vith. Hitler's counteroffensive faced the danger of stalling. The main weight of the assault shifted onto Wehrmacht and SS units in the south where seven critically important roads, like spokes on a wheel, lead from Bastogne—one of them heading directly toward the port city of Antwerp, the German prime objective. Tanks and infantry converged on Bastogne, seeking to crush the thin American defenses there, capture the vital roads, rush to the sea and cut off the northern Allied armies.

CHAPTER ELEVEN

Outside Bastogne

December 20, 1944

Wilcox

Journal entry for Wednesday, December 20th:

Chilled to the bone. A heavy mist today on the woods and fields. The Krauts are out there now. We clashed with one of their patrols northeast of here last night and captured three of their wounded. This morning they probed this way again as far as the farm across the field. We sat tight and let our mortars deal with them. Later we headed out on another patrol, doing a little probing of our own, but the Krauts had withdrawn.

The rumbles in the distance indicate the big action right now is southwest of us, back the way we rode in. Our sector up here is fairly quiet, although we can occasionally hear their trucks or tanks in the distance, and once in a while, we get a dose of their artillery.

A Black artillery sergeant came through with a detail laying field telephone wire and checking the effect of the barrage on the Solvay Farm. He confirmed rumors that the Germans have cut us off.

The African-American artillerymen came by in the morning, stringing wire along the MLR— Main Line of Resistance—and hooking up field telephones between the Lieutenant and his squads and their observation posts strung-out along the ridge-line. Rumors of the tactical situation had filtered through from neighboring units. The squad shared lukewarm coffee with the detail and pounced on the crusty old artillery sergeant for any information breaking their feeling of isolation.

"Tell it to you all straight, as much as I know," the sergeant said. "We're like the hole in a donut, cut-off in a pocket about 5 miles across. Inside the pocket are most of your division, parts of two armored combat commands, plus a few odds and ends from retreating units that didn't make it out in time, like the guns from my outfit. Your division's in overall command."

Nurnberg piped up, "Well, shouldn't we be able to handle this? Isn't the airborne supposed to drop in the enemy's rear areas and operate with little support?"

"Yeah, 'cept this time the rear area came to us," Cooper said.

Wilcox asked, "You've been around the pocket, how do you think we're set for this fight?"

"We've got plenty of big guns, but few shells," the sergeant continued, "little food and small weapons ammo, but orders are to hold at all costs. Tankers have formed a "fire brigade" to rush out wherever a hot spot develops. Hope that works."

"Me too, said Wilcox. "Any other bad news?"

"Krauts captured the field hospital when they sealed us off, so we're short on doctors and medical supplies. Wounded are piling up in the basements back in town. If we live through this, we'll all be famous or on our way to a German P.O.W. camp."

"I'll pick 'famous,' if I have to choose," said Cooper.

"And thanks for the coffee," the sergeant said. "You'll hear soon that rations are being cut. This may be the last coffee we all see for a long time."

* * * * * * *

The weather grew even worse, and the suffering on the line increased, the beginning of the worst European winter in almost forty years. During the night of December 21st, six to twelve inches of snow fell. The temperature plunged close to zero degrees Fahrenheit; during the day, it barely rose above freezing.

Short on other food, the company's cooks could only offer the men boiled white beans and plain pancakes, utilizing the only other food stockpiled in town, to supplement what rations the division brought with them. None of the chow reached the front lines warm.

Rushed to the battle without any winter clothing or equipment, the men's suffering increased. Facing immediate combat, the men had dropped off their packs and bedrolls before passing through Bastogne. The encircling enemy captured these. Troopers faced a critical shortage of sleeping bags and blankets.

Out on the line, the defenders had little shelter and no fires. Men slept in frozen holes in the ground and carried their canteens inside their shirts to keep water from freezing. Runners brought bed sheets and towels from town out to the lines for warmth and camouflage, but not enough to go around. Some men wrapped their boots in burlap sacking, but this had to be done with care or the material soaked up melt water from the snow and made their feet even colder. Frostbite and trench foot became a major concern.

Despite the cold and lack of food, the men struggled to maintain their fighting spirit. Although their lived in the same dirty uniforms day after day, most men on the line somehow contrived to remain clean-shaven in defiance of their situation. However, all the spirit and determination in the world eventually wear down when things only change for the worse, when scarce resources run out and when a tenacious foe's continued assaults use up already depleted ammunition and manpower.

* * * * * * *

The squad improved their position, re-stacking stones from the wall by the O.P., making firing platforms for the machine gun and bazooka crews and creating a stile for easier movement over the wall. They dug a slit trench behind the wall to aid in defending their front if enemy vehicles approached. They laid logs and a layer of dirt over the O.P. foxhole for protection from mortar fire. The men cut other pine branches, fashioning simple roofs over their foxholes, providing some protection from the weather and for camouflage. They laid more branches down inside for insulation from the frozen ground.

Even with improvements and men doubling up in the foxholes, sharing body heat, the cold prevented much sleep. Constant shivering wore down reserves of energy. Food supplies ran short. Rations were cut and cut again.

The Captain or the company executive officer inspected the line every day. The Lieutenant and Reynolds alternated in regular rounds, checking on the physical welfare of their men, position of weapons and defenses, fields of fire, and available ammo. It pained the leaders that they couldn't do more for their men's comfort or the supply situation.

When the line seemed quiet, the Lieutenant had Wilcox rotate his squad in two-man, two-hour shifts down to the observation post. He permitted each pair rotating off to retire back beyond next ridge and warm up at the aid station for twenty minutes, a chance to dry their feet and wash and dry their socks to prevent trench foot. Coffee nonexistent, and even the thinnest broth scarce, melted snow heated by the aid station fire became a welcome warm beverage. Any fires closer to the line would attract unwanted attention. Enemy patrols might not see the flames, but they would smell the smoke and direct artillery towards the source.

When not on watch or patrol, the men slept in pairs in their foxholes on the slope of the ridge, backs together, huddled together for what warmth they could share. When not asleep, they passed the time out under the canopy of the pines talking of home.

"All this fresh air is killin; me," Cooper moaned through chattering teeth. "Never this cold back in Brooklyn. I can barely feel my toes."

"When it became this cold back home, I used to beg my uncle to take me ice fishing with him on Lake Winnebago," Nurnberg said.

"Did he catch much ice?" Cooper quipped.

"Very funny." Nurnberg continued, "Bitter cold sometimes out on the lake, but at least we had an ice shanty to cut the wind and keep out the snow."

"I'd go for an ice shanty or any other kind right now," Wilcox said. He sniffled and glanced around him at the snow-frosted pine branches. "This cold has my nose running like a faucet."

"I'd just go for a cup of hot chocolate," said Anderson, "like we used to have after ice skating in the village park back home." Although awed by his first experience being in a combat zone, and facing the same discomfort and shortages as the rest of the men, he maintained a cheerful attitude.

"Yeah," said Nurnberg. "Even without whipped cream."

Cooper stirred at something in his mess cup. "You know, if you mix this K-Ration lemonade powder with the snow, it makes a tolerable dessert!"

"Just what we need in this weather—lemon ice!" Wilcox said, sniffling again and shaking his head in disbelief.

"Momma ever tell ya *not* to eat yellow snow?" asked Vincenti.

"Wish we had one of Friedenfeld's fruitcakes right now," Nurnberg said. "Whatever did he do with them?"

"Left 'em in a sack beneath his bunk back in camp," Vincenti said.

"At least something we left behind won't be looted while we're gone," Wilcox said.

Nurnberg said, "I know what we need. We need this weather to break."

"Then planes could drop us some supplies," Joe said.

"And drop some stuff on those Krauts," added Cooper.

Burnanski had been suffering like the rest of them, but his brooding kept him silent most of the morning. "Haven't you prayed about it, kid?" he sneered. "Maybe your God isn't listening to you right now. If He cared for you, why'd He let you get into this mess?"

"Maybe so I could be here with you," Joe said.

Burnanski returned to his brooding.

"What's your historical perspective on our sitchy-ation, Perfesser?" Cooper asked. "G.I.'s ever had it this bad in a past war?"

"You really want to know?" asked Wilcox.

"Sure," Cooper said. "Doubt if history'll make me feel warmer, but lay it out. Know you're dyin' to tell us."

"Well," said Wilcox. "The way I figure it, not since Valley Forge have so many American fighting men suffered so much in cold weather during a war. And in some ways we have it worse."

"Think so?" asked Vincenti. "Valley Forge isn't far from Philly. Went out there on a field trip once, but in the spring."

"Yeah, I've been there too. I've thought back on everything I've read about it," Wilcox said. 'Had it bad back then, but men at Valley Forge didn't face snipers, mines and artillery. They could light warming fires, had built log huts to sleep in, and could move about freely. But no supplies got through. No food, shoes, or winter clothing. No medical supplies."

"What caused that?" Nurnberg asked.

"The British captured Philadelphia and New York City," Wilcox said.

"Even Brooklyn!" Cooper said proudly. "Remember that from grammar school."

"Philly, I can understand," said Vincenti. "But Brooklyn?"

"Yeah, even Brooklyn," Cooper said. "Red Coats controlled both sides of the East River that way."

Wilcox continued, "The British occupation disrupted the flow of supplies, which hadn't been great even before that. Congress had fled west into Pennsylvania, and disorganization increased, so Washington finally dispatched one of his top aides, Nathaniel Greene, to straighten out the supply problem."

"Wish somebody'd straighten out ours," Nurnberg said.

"There's a story about Washington praying in the snow at that time," Joe said. "Might only be a legend, but things did improve. I'm praying they'll improve for us too."

"Keep the prayers going," Wilcox said.

"Yeah, kid," Cooper said. "Keep sending 'em up."

"I will," said Joe."

* * * * * * *

North, south and west beyond Bastogne, the intense battle in the Ardennes raged on. As news reached home, the American public began realizing the extreme gravity of the situation. In churches, factories, and homes, prayers began to be offered around the clock for the soldiers in the battle.

* * * * * * *

THE ANDERSONS

Back in Illinois, Susan Anderson stood inside the village park district's boathouse with a group of friends. They were enjoying themselves at an after school, early holiday skating party on Lake Ellyn in the park below the high school. Several dozen skaters outside continued circling around the frozen surface of the lake under the streetlights as winter twilight fell on the scene. Inside the boathouse, excitement about the approach of Christmas vacation in a few days tinged the happy chatter of teenagers and grade school children. Warming themselves before a cozy fire burning in the large field-stone fireplace, the young people enjoyed hot cider, donuts and fresh popcorn. From a radio behind the snack bar came the mingled voices of Bing Crosby and the Henderson Choir singing from a new recording of the wartime hit song "I'll be Home for Christmas."

The radio programming transitioned from music to a commercial for a Chicagoland upholstery and rug cleaner, followed by national and international news. The lead story reported the war in Europe and a German breakthrough in Belgium. Other young people continued their hubbub of happy talk, but Susan Anderson's attention focused on the broadcast. She bid farewell to her friends and buttoned up her coat. She tied the laces of her white figure skates together and slung the pair over her shoulder. Streetlights guided her up the fresh-plowed streets.

After arriving home, Susan sat with her mother in their living room knitting some hand-made Christmas presents. Susan kept thinking about the news bulletin she'd heard earlier. The more she thought about it, the more she worried. She wrung her hands for the umpteenth time and rubbed them along her skirt. "Joe's in that battle I heard about, I just know it," she said to her mother.

Mrs. Anderson stopped her knitting. Her spirit had also begun stirring with urgency about Joe's safety. She peered over her glasses at her daughter. "Worrying won't help him or us either," she said, forcing herself to sound calm. "I believe the best we can do for him is pray."

The two women set aside their yarn and bowed their heads together.

"Dear Heavenly Father," Mrs. Anderson began. "We thank You that You know exactly where Joe is right now. He may be in a desperate battle. Keep him safe and help him perform his duty. We know that he battles for men's souls as well. Work in the hearts of the soldiers he's with. Help Your gospel light to shine through Joe. We pray especially for whichever man is farthest from Your light, that Joe might lead him to that light. Grant Joe Your protection, Your grace, and Your power. We ask this in Jesus' name, Amen."

Susan Anderson stood and turned to the window. She gazed out past the paper snowflake decorations hanging there. More real snow fell in the darkness outside. The flakes falling closest to the window illuminated for a moment by the light inside as they fell past. "Seems like we'll have a cold winter this year," she said to herself. "Wondered if it's as cold and snowy where Joe is."

* * * * * * *

Joe Anderson ducked under a low-hanging pine branch. He shivered as a clump of snow fell onto the exposed back of his neck. He trudged through a dark, snowy forest five paces behind Wilcox on patrol. Burnanski acted as the scout, about twenty-five paces further ahead, breaking a path wherever the forest opened and deeper patches of snow lay. Wilcox kept Anderson and his new-found B.A.R. up front behind Burnanski and himself, and then Tobin next to Friedenfeld bringing up the rear.

Until they proved themselves, Wilcox never sent more than two of the new men out at a time and kept them near veterans. Because of Burnanski's attitude, and concerned for Anderson's safety, Wilcox never left them alone together. In a squad as small as his, contact between the men was unavoidable, but out on a patrol or back in the bivouac, if Burnanski and Anderson were both there, either Wilcox or Cooper was there as well. He hoped the situation would blow over, but kept a close personal eye on it for now. Anderson 's position, relatively close to Burnanski, on this patrol came because tactics dictated the automatic weapon at the head of the group, ready to swing into action if they came into trouble. With Burnanski leading twenty paces out front, Wilcox next in line, and the need for silence, little opportunity for any friction existed between the two for the time being.

Like dealing with a troublesome school bully, Wilcox thought.

The sun set that day around 4:00 local time. An earlier patrol by Sgt. Herdlika's neighboring squad headed out soon after, seeking to capture two or three Germans for interrogation. Herdlika's group skirmished with an opposing patrol, returning after four hours, empty handed with two of their men wounded. Division intelligence, desperate for information about enemy activity and intentions on this quarter of the perimeter, pressed for another patrol. Now Wilcox's squad bore the burden for completing the task out in the cold and fog. At least the cover of darkness aided them, plenty of it under overcast skies and with the approaching sunrise at that latitude and season not coming until after 8:30 A.M. The waxing quarter moon had set just before the sun did the previous afternoon and wouldn't rise again until after dawn. Perfect cover for a long night patrol.

Wilcox assigned Burnanski the familiar role of scout and "Kraut hunter." Success as an undersized unit depended on his experience and skill. He seemed to be able to lay aside his sullen isolation when called on for such duty. More pressing, present-time factors occupied his thoughts as he tuned his senses to the danger. They slipped out before midnight, combed the dark, foggy woods south of the Solvay's farm, but so far turned up nothing. The earlier patrol obscured whatever tracks Germans may have left there. Burnanski suggested shifting their patrol north and east.

Casting out in a wide arc, Burnanski led them farther and farther away from their own position, crossing fog-veiled fields and patches of forest in between, toward ruins of a neighboring farmhouse. They found many tracks from German activity. One set made after the most recent snowfall appeared to be tracks from a ten-man *Streife*, or squad, possibly out on patrol themselves, maybe the same ones who'd tangled earlier with Herdlika's patrol. The tracks emerged from a large eastern forest area and followed a regular path crossing a plowed field heading west toward the American positions.

Wilcox halted the patrol at the edge of an old growth forest, sending Burnanski into the trees scouting for any German presence down the narrow, winding trail the Streife had used. The other men spread out, listening into the foggy night for sounds of the enemy.

Tobin's boot kicked against something flat covered with snow. He felt its shape and whispered to Wilcox, "Some sort of sign lying in the snow."

Wilcox lifted the sign on its fallen post, turned it over and brushed off the snow. He shielded his flashlight, took a quick look. On the sign read, *"Aucune Infraction! Belge National Réserve Forestière. Pas de Chasse sans Permis!"* He clicked the light off.

"What's it say?" Tobin whispered.

"Says, 'No Trespassing! Belgian National Forest Reserve. No Hunting without Permission.'" Wilcox whispered. He put his hand on Tobin's shoulder. "Don't think that applies to us."

Friedenfeld came running over. "I hear Krauts coming across the snow from the southeast!"

"Into the forest!" Wilcox ordered, leading the way. Within the old-growth forest, trees varied in size: Many thick, towering pines with narrow saplings and scattered brush beneath their canopy. The randomly spaced trees grew further apart, unlike the orderly rows back at their own encampment, allowing more light beneath, and a lot of dead-fall timbers lay about. The trail snaked and curved through all this on its way east. Burnanski returned, coming back the other way, and reported no German activity for at least 200 yards father along the trail.

Seizing the opportunity for ambush, Wilcox deployed his men a short distance within the forest, along a curving section of the trail where dead-falls created a small clearing. They could wait under cover there and catch the Streife approaching from the west. What light available in that moonless night penetrated beneath the forest canopy at this open area, and the fog thinned out. Friedenfeld prepared a position behind cover off the northern side of the trail. Wilcox set Anderson and Tobin behind a large fallen log on the southern side. Burnanski would take his position farther east down the trail, dealing with any scouts the others let past and ready to close in if needed.

Wilcox briefed the others with his impromptu strategy: Any German scouts would be allowed to pass by along the trail unmolested. Burnanski would deal with them if it came to a fight. If they were only a Streife, his patrol would attack. If they were a larger group, too big for an ambush, the patrol would let them pass. If they were a Streife on patrol, when the leaders of the main body came within point blank range abreast of Wilcox and the two rookies' positions things would start. Friedenfeld, from behind cover, would call out a warning for the Streife to drop weapons and put their hands up. After calling that warning, he would shift position, rolling to his immediate right behind cover. If the main Streife opened fire at the sound of Friedenfeld's warning, he wouldn't be where they heard his voice. Because of the curve in the trail, he would also be out of Wilcox, Anderson and Tobin's direct line of fire, and they would be out of his, but the enemy would be exposed from both directions.

Only a remote possibility existed that all the Germans would surrender without resistance, so Wilcox, his mind racing ahead, prepared for the opposite. *Comes to a fight,* he reminded himself, *five tasks ahead.* The first task would be neutralizing the Streife by taking out its leadership and its three-man light machine gun team, the most dangerous part of a German infantry squad. The second task would be preventing escape by any of the enemy: Eliminating the head and tail of the Streife's column would aid in confining the remainder to the ambush zone. The third task would be overwhelming and disarming the survivors and guarding against tricks. The fourth task would be securing prisoners, gathering maps and other significant material. The fifth task would be a swift get-away before other German forces, alerted by gunfire or grenades, converged on the scene.

Wilcox whispered target assignments to Anderson and Tobin, who lay behind the fallen log about five paces apart, fifteen yards off the trail, with clear lanes of fire through the trees. With the light so dim, he told them to aim low at the enemy muzzle blasts if it came to shooting. He reminded them about keeping one eye closed while firing so that eye would retain night vision and not be blinded by the flash of weapons. He also instructed them to keep weapons on safety until Friedenfeld called and wait for himself to open fire first. He wanted no premature shooting. The goal was capturing prisoners, so he'd give the Germans that much of a chance to come out alive. Time raced by, but he reviewed instructions and procedure with the new men, making each repeat everything back. If things went wrong, they would fall back west and reassemble to the right of the trail at the near edge of the smaller forest across the field. If they became separated, each should keep off forest trails, strike south to the creek and follow its ravine west back to their lines, wary of possible enemy positions along the way.

Wilcox scraped away snow, twigs and pine cones, preparing his own hasty position behind another tree five paces to Anderson's right. His primary target would be the German patrol leader, usually next in line behind any scouts. Tobin would begin firing at the last person in the Streife, working his way in to the next in line. Anderson, in the middle with his automatic weapon, received the task of taking out the gunner, loader and ammo carrier of the Streife's light machine gun crew. The crewmen were usually the next behind the leader, ready for immediate deployment. If the Streife hit the dirt, Joe would then fire short bursts, back and forth above them, keeping the remaining Germans down until Wilcox or Friedenfeld determined that any survivors had ceased resistance, leaving two or three to capture and return for interrogation.

A cold, tense wait from behind cover replaced the few minutes of preparation activity. Wilcox's eye began twitching again, and his lower back gave spasmodic protest about his crouching posture. Burnanski and Friedenfeld waited at the forest edge, watching and listening into the fog for the Germans approaching across the field.

Hope these Krauts think they're in the clear after they cross the field and let down their guard, Wilcox thought. *At least we should have advantages of surprise and more time for night vision to adjust within these darker woods.*

Burnanski's ears picked up the faint clatter of German field gear. He nudged Friedenfeld, who alerted Wilcox, as Burnanski slipped through the trees to his position down the trail. As instructed, the two rookies double-checked their weapons and waited for Friedenfeld to call out his warning and Wilcox to open fire if a fight came.

Ten enemy soldiers trudged back from their patrol, retracing their path through the fog and across the snowy field, into the old growth forest. In the middle of the group, two of them pulled a sled laden with a long bundle. The Streife had been strung out, five paces between each man, in the open field. Two *Späher*, or scouts, led the way. The first one continued ahead on the path into the forest. Light would be even dimmer once they came into the trees, so the second Späher waited as the Streife bunched up behind him so they could keep each other in sight. As they entered the woods and approached Wilcox's hidden men in the gloomy clearing, the Germans' white snow smocks stood out in contrast with the dark forest growth around them.

Perfect, thought Wilcox. *Just what we want.* He released the safety on his submachine gun.

One of the Germans towing the sled sighed, saying to his comrades, "Endlich wieder in den Bäumen und die Heimat warme Decke."

"Stille, bis die Patrouille ist fertig!" scolded one near the head of the Streife.

Wilcox took aim at the last speaker as he came abreast.

Friedenfeld shouted, "Hände hoch! Lassen Sie Ihre Waffen! Sie sind Ungeben!"

The men in the Streife dropped to the trail around the sled. Some crouched. Some lay prone.

Krak! Krak! Their rifles opened fire toward Friedenfeld's voice.

Wilcox answered with fire of his own—one short burst on the crouching patrol leader. Wilcox swung right with two short bursts, emptying his magazine on the second Späher before the leader fell over into the snow.

Brrrrrrrrrip! The Streife's machine gunner began firing to his right. An erratic burst ripped through tree branches above Wilcox and Anderson's heads. This fire cut short as Anderson's B.A.R. rattled short bursts down low, silencing the crew and their weapon.

Tobin's carbine snapped four close-range shots into the rear of the group, taking out the last two men in line. Burnanski's rifle barked twice off to the right down the trail. Friedenfeld's shots cracked from the left. The confused remainder of the Streife fired left and right toward Friedenfeld or Anderson. Bullets gouged chunks of bark off the huge tree where Friedenfeld squatted out of sight.

A machine pistol sprayed in the opposite direction, above where

Joe Anderson lay in a depression behind the log. Chunks of pine branches and clumps of snow fell. Joe poked his weapon through a space beneath the log, firing a few short bursts over the heads of the enemy.

As Joe reloaded, Friedenfeld shouted, "Sie sind umzingelt! Feuer einstellen! Sie sind umgeben. Hände hoch!"

The Germans stopped firing. One raised his hands.

"Cease fire!" Wilcox called to Joe and Tobin.

The stillness of the forest returned, now an odd contrast to the short violent noise of the ambush. Acrid smoke hung in the air. A murmur of German voices broke the momentary silence, cut short by a guttural command. The Steife's survivor with his hands above his head stood and shouted, "Komeraade!" Another one pulled him down and slapped him.

"Werfen Sie Ihre Arme! Aufstehen! Nehmen Sie Ihre Gurte!" called Friedenfeld.

"Watch for tricks!" Wilcox said, stepping into the open with his gun poised waist high.

The first man stood again, leaving his rifle in the snow, taking off his outer belt. The one who slapped him tossed away his machine pistol. A third also stood with his hands up.

Wilcox approached the three Germans. Friedenfeld emerged on the opposite side of the group. The second German turned his body away, appearing to release an outer equipment belt while pulling the arming cord on a *Stielhandgranat*, a "potato masher" stick grenade, tucked beneath his snow smock. Friedenfeld, wary of such tricks, shot the man before he could throw it. The Stielhandgranat dropped beside the sled. The man's body fell on top of it.

Friedenfeld shouted, "Live grenade!"

Everyone in the open hit the snow. The third German bolted off into the trees, whipped around and fired a semi-automatic pistol. Erratic bullets zipped past Friedenfeld and Wilcox. Wilcox swung his gun up, dropping the shooter with a short burst. The grenade exploded. The dead man's body shielded others from the direct blast, but his blood splattered surrounding snow and one side of the sled.

"What's that sled carrying?" Friedenfeld asked, seeing the mess around it.

"A wounded man they were transporting back," Wilcox said.

"Bitte! Bitte! Nicht schießen! Nicht schießen!" pleaded a remaining live German lying beyond the sled on the trail, the one who'd originally put his hands up.

Friedenfeld poked the warm muzzle of his rifle in the back of the soldier's exposed neck and said, "Aufstehen! Aus mit dem Gürtel! Hände hinter den Kopf! Schnell!

The soldier, a large teenager, broke into tears. He rose, finished taking off his belt and placed his hands behind his head as ordered. Friedenfeld patted him down and removed bayonet, clasp knife and other articles. He tugged the boy aside and stood him facing a tree.

Wilcox and Anderson checked the other bodies lying in the snow. All were dead.

Joe and Tobin kept guard while Wilcox and Friedenfeld searched the remaining living and the dead, gathering assorted knives, pistols, *Soldbücher* pay books and anything else of possible military value. Wilcox dumped out a German ammo haversack and stuffed the booty inside the bag for examination in detail later. He pocketed a pair of field-glasses, thinking, *These will come in handy in our own observation post.*

Friedenfeld gathered German grenades and rations into another haversack. Wilcox sent Anderson to check the condition of the wounded man on the sled, while he smashed the Streife's light machine gun against a tree.

Burnanski arrived before Anderson at the place where the wounded German lay upon the sled. The helmetless soldier remained alive, breathing out in heavy gasps, face screwed up from pain, holding his bandaged right side. The man spit in contempt at Burnanski, who kicked the spittle-covered snow back at the man. Burnanski raised his M-1, aimed at the man's exposed head and squeezed off a shot.

The rifle clicked on a jammed chamber.

While Burnanski cursed and withdrew the malfunctioning clip, Joe Anderson stepped in between him and the wounded man. Joe knelt and pulled up the soldier's snow smock. He opened the man's field jacket and began examining his wounded side, arm and bandaged leg by flashlight.

Burnanski cursed again, reversing his weapon and raising it to club Anderson's head with the butt.

"None of that in my squad, 'Ski!" Wilcox said through gritted teeth. "Go watch down the trail!"

Burnanski turned, kicking snow on Anderson and the prisoner in the process. He trotted off into the woods.

The German struggled through his pain to pull his service pistol from its holster. Joe jerked the man's hand away and pocketed the weapon. The German spit in Joe's face. Joe yanked the snow smock higher, covering the man's head, and wiped his face with a sleeve. The man struggled against Joe, squirming and pushing Joe away while he attempted to examine and treat the wounds, spewing out a stream of German insults from beneath the smock. "Schießen, mich jetzt, Ungeziefer Feigling!"

"How is he, Anderson?" Wilcox asked.

"In pain and feisty. Keeps pushing me away and cussing up a storm."

"We'll fix that," Wilcox said. He pulled out lengths of paracord brought along for securing prisoners. He bound the man's hands together and stretched out the wounded prisoner's arms above the prisoner's head, tying them to the rear of the sled.

The wounded man spat toward Wilcox as well, growling, "Dreckigen Hände von mir, Schwein Amerikaner!"

"Fix that too," Wilcox said. He yanked out a field bandage and gagged the man. "How bad is he hurt?"

"Took a couple slugs earlier through his upper right leg. No arterial bleeding. Another bullet grazed his right arm and opened the muscle on his right side, but not penetrating his liver or intestines, from what I can tell. They did a hurried job patching him up. Replaced a bandage with one from my kit," Joe said.

"You do that pretty good. You train as a medic?"

"Boy Scouts," Joe said. "With the war on, scout leaders emphasized first aid. Mine served as a medic in the 1st Division during the last war and later became my high school biology teacher. He knew his stuff." Joe uncovered the wounded man's insignia. "This guy's a '*Leutnant*' or whatever they call them in the SS."

"An *Obersturmführer*," Wilcox said. "The man who pulled the grenade was SS too. A *Scharführer*, as far as I can tell from what's left of him, one of their SS non-com ranks. Maybe this guy's assistant. The others all look to be regular Wehrmacht Landsers."

"The officer carried this inside his snow smock" Anderson handed a thick, folded map to Wilcox.

"Bet he and his sergeant went out gathering intelligence of their own. Guessing they're part of the Kraut patrol the other squad tangled with earlier tonight. Lost a couple men themselves and were hauling this wounded officer back on a supply sled."

"Think we should bring this guy in? We can use their sled. I'll pull it. Make the unwounded prisoner help."

"Risky and slow us way down in this snow," Wilcox said to himself, thinking aloud. "Was thinking of ditching him here, but he'd be a prize if we can drag him in. Can always dump him if we run into trouble." He made up his mind and gave orders. "All right, everyone, on the double! Friedenfeld, rig a couple of their stick grenades across the trail to slow pursuers from the east. Anderson, pack that guy up for transport and tie him in. Tobin, keep your barrel poking the other prisoner's neck. I'll clean up some of our mess." Wilcox tossed Wehrmacht first aid kit onto the snow beside Joe. "Give the officer a shot of their morphine to quiet him down for the trip back."

Tobin guarded the teenaged Landser facing the tree. Anderson finished bundling up the wounded officer. Wilcox tossed weapons far into the brush.

Using a trick learned from the Germans during house to house fighting back in Holland, Friedenfeld improvised a booby trap where the path narrowed between two large pines. He tied the grenades to the trees on either side of the narrow place and rigged another length of paracord as a trip line between them. The grenades would explode moments after pulling their friction wires. Friedenfeld waited for Burnanski's retrun before setting the rigged grenades.

"Got an idea. Help me with these bodies before they freeze up," Wilcox said to Friedenfeld. "Strip off their snow gear and spread them out behind some trees as decoys."

Wilcox and Friedenfeld dragged the dead bodies to either side of the trail.

"Something from a history book?" Friedenfeld asked.

"Nah, saw this in a cheap Western once," Wilcox explained. "Fooled some Hollywood bad guys."

They deposited them behind scattered trees and propped them up visible to the trail.

"If your booby trap blows, maybe these bodies will make 'em think they've come upon us waiting behind the trees," Wilcox said. "Might delay a Kraut patrol for a few extra minutes here in the gloom."

"Might," Friedenfeld said. "Better than leaving our handiwork lying all over the trail."

Wilcox relieved Tobin and sent him to help Friedenfeld in tossing German helmets and other remaining gear into the trees and kicking clean snow over blood, the grenade blast mark and other obvious signs of the fight. Wilcox directed the uninjured prisoner over to the sled. Anderson guarded him while Wilcox made the teenaged Landser put his belt back on, freeing his hands for pulling the sled. Wilcox tied a longer length of paracord to the back of the teen's belt and loosely to sled. No way the Landser could bolt off without untying the paracord first.

Morphine had yet to take full effect. The officer's gag had loosened, and he awoke, crying out in pain as they moved him. Wilcox adjusted the gag, muffling further cries. Joe rolled up a snow smock and tucked it under the officer's head to cushion it during the bumpy ride ahead.

Burnanski hurried back with word that a platoon or more of Germans approached in a skirmish line, probing along either side of the forest trail less than three hundred yards east. Friedenfeld set his trap. He scraped together a ridge of snow and pine needles to conceal the trip line.

"Move out!" Wilcox said. Burnanski trotted on ahead. Wilcox and the sled pullers followed next. Joe had the longer rope and took the lead in towing, followed by the Landser a few feet behind. Tobin followed close behind the sled, keeping guard on both Germans and helping Joe tug the sled over rough places. Friedenfeld watched a few paces to the rear. The whole ambush and aftermath in the pre-dawn woods had taken over twenty minutes. *More time than I wished, but we've bagged our game*, thought Wilcox. *Hope it's worth it.*

Wilcox's patrol passed through the fog across the first open field and entered cover of the forest strip beyond. They emerged onto another fog-shrouded, snowy field on the far side.

Kraak! Kraak! Friedenfeld's double-grenade booby trap exploded in the distant pines. Scattered gunfire followed as nervous Germans opened fire on the dark forms of supposed enemy soldiers lurking behind trees in the forest shadows.

Burnanski led them on at a fast pace. Dawn had come before they reached the far side of the Solvay farm, but fog and low clouds continued casting a twilight pall over the early morning countryside, screening them from view. Wilcox sent Burnanski running on ahead, alerting Cooper and the others that the patrol returned to their lines with prisoners. He wanted no friendly-fire accident erasing all their risk and effort.

The Lieutenant arrived with a couple men from Herdlika's squad as the remaining patrol came around the roadblock mines. "How'd it go?" he asked.

"We bagged two from a returning Kraut patrol," Wilcox said. "Maybe from the same group that tangled with our earlier patrol. One of the prisoners is a wounded Obersturmführer. The other's a teen-aged Wehrmacht private. The rest were regular Landsers too, except for a non-com who pulled a grenade on us when we took them prisoner. Friedenfeld plugged him. He fell onto his own grenade."

The Lieutenant nodded, mentally picturing the results of falling on a German grenade.

"Thinking maybe this Obersturmführer's one of their *Nachrichtenoffizieres* out getting a firsthand look. He carried this map," Wilcox said, handing the captured map to the Lieutenant.

"An intelligence officer? Excellent!" said the Lieutenant, glancing at the map, but could only detect its size and shape in the dim light. "And your men, any wounded?"

"Cold, hungry and tired, but otherwise intact."

"Great! How did the rookies do?"

"Kept quiet, obeyed orders, killed Krauts. Everything you'd want from them," Wilcox said.

"Good to hear," the Lieutenant said. "You can give me a detailed report in a moment. Cooper, take these two from Herdlika's squad. Relieve Anderson and Tobin with those prisoners, and hustle that sled over to the aid station. S-2 will deal with the Krauts from there. Hand them this map."

"Yes, sir!" Cooper said.

"Thank you, men, for a job well done!" the Lieutenant said to Wilcox's patrol.

After Wilcox had given the Lieutenant a complete account of the patrol, he sat down with Anderson, Tobin and Friedenfeld. Burnanski sat by himself a couple yards away. Winding down from all the tension and activity, they shared a skimpy breakfast supplemented with some of the *Eiserne Portionen*, or "iron rations," captured from the Streife—*Fleishkonserve*, a canned meat of unknown content, and *Knackebrot*, hard whole wheat crackers. They topped the crackers with *Schmelzkäse*, a processed cheese confiscated from the SS-Obersturmführer, which squeezed like toothpaste out of metal tubes.

Knowing that new men are often shaken up after killing enemy soldiers for the first time, especially at such close range, Wilcox checked on their state. Both Tobin and Anderson had been quiet. Tobin rubbed his neck and glanced from place to place. Anderson sat with his head down, looking at his food with dull, wet eyes. Wilcox rubbed his twitching eye and asked, "What do you new guys think about what happened on patrol? You killed your first enemy up close and touched their dead and wounded afterward."

Tobin's Adam's apple bobbed. "Everything happened so fast," he said. "I shot two guys; then it was all over."

"Short and violent, the usual way of these things," Wilcox said.

"Too busy to think much about it until we got away over the second field," said Anderson.

"Also part of it," Wilcox said. "Training kicks in. Do your job, think about it later."

Burnanski leaned over and sneered, "Well, Reverend, were you *praying* before you killed those Krauts?!" His sarcasm shredded the calm atmosphere Wilcox sought.

Joe Anderson regarded him for a moment and said, "Yes, I was."

Burnanski snorted. "I thought the Bible says, "Thou shalt not kill!"

"It does," Joe said, "but that refers to deliberate murder."

Tobin leaned forward and asked "What about killing men in a war?"

All the others perked up, even Burnanski, at what the Holy Joe would say. Cooper, returning from the aid station, paused to listen as well.

"I struggled with the idea of killing the enemy, and gave it much thought and prayer before I joined up," said Anderson. "The Lord led me to the conclusion that what I do as a soldier is in the service of my country, an extension of that authority, represented by this uniform I wear. The deaths of my country's enemies on this morning's patrol weren't a result of personal, selfish hate. I won't go soft on the enemy, wary for tricks. But if given a chance for doing good toward them, to 'love my enemies,' showing human decency, I will, like I did treating the wounds of that officer we captured. I know those opportunities are rare. In battle, it mostly comes down to kill or be killed, and the United States Government authorizes me to kill that others might live, for as long as I'm in this war."

"Well put, 'Sgt. York,'" said Cooper, popping in another toothpick.

"So you don't take moral responsibility for those you kill?" Wilcox asked.

"My responsibility is in obeying those appointed over me. Moral responsibility in this war rests on our government, whether it's on the side of what's right with God or not. It's clear that Hitler and those bound to him are evil. The Nazis won't hesitate in killing innocent people, like they've done in bombing whole cities, gunning down civilians in reprisals, or what they might do to my mom and sister back home if they ever got to them. Because of that, I won't hesitate in stopping the forces of evil and their atrocities. Their shed blood stains the hands of Hitler and his cohorts, not mine."

Wilcox lifted an eyebrow. "Surely you feel some emotion about killing those men today."

"Anger and sorrow," Joe said, tears filling his eyes again. "Angry at their wicked leaders and their twisted ideology for making me have to kill those men, and sorrow for souls I may have sent on to a Christless eternity. I didn't enjoy it. I did what I had to do for the patrol, this squad, my country and my family, and I'm ready to go on doing it if that's what it takes to wipe out the evil and end this awful war."

Burnanski grimaced, rose, and walked off to his foxhole and lay down, out of sight, pondering what Joe had said. Others from the patrol drifted off to their foxholes as well, seeking some rest.

Tobin paused by Anderson and put a hand on his shoulder "Thanks, Joe. Relieves my mind, hearing you share all that."

Friedenfeld leaned over toward Joe and whispered as he passed by. "Mine too."

Mine too, thought Wilcox.

CHAPTER TWELVE

Northeast of Bastogne

December 22, 1944

Wilcox

Journal entry for Thursday, December 21:

> *No more snow so far today but more fog, overcast skies, and German artillery. We're all terribly cold. Everyone is on edge from the tension and the cold—seems to be no escape from either. I don't think I've slept more than a few minutes at a stretch. Same with the other guys. We massage our feet to keep blood circulating and beat our arms across our chests in the "teamster's warm-up," but we're constantly chilled. Any physical exertion brings on a sweat that freezes and makes us colder still.*

> *We sit around in frozen misery unless slogging around on patrol, which has deadly hazards of its own. We stumble through the snow, forest or fog and quickly lose orientation. Pine branches and snow dampen sounds, so in seconds a man can break contact with the squad or even guy next to him. We lose all sense of direction with the gray sky, the fog, the falling snow, and the thick branches of the fir trees.*

> *Death always waits out there Sometimes we don't know where the enemy is until almost on top of him. Sometimes we smell him, by his tobacco and leather, before we see him. Every step might draw fire from the enemy or some trigger-happy friend. The enemy has set mines out there now, easily hidden in the snow.*

We captured an SS intelligence officer while out on patrol. Our interrogators gleaned some important information from him and a map he'd been marking. Because of that, most of the squad is heading out tonight on a special long-range patrol. All signs hint at a dangerous mission, yet anything seems better than sitting around here and doing nothing but freezing.

Mom and Dad, I've written more than I should, if this journal's ever captured, but I wanted you to know where I was heading into if I don't come back and always remember that I love you.

The Lieutenant handpicked the long-range patrol's members from Wilcox's men, the only one of his squads yet unscathed. He chose combat veterans Friedenfeld and Vincenti, and Wilcox as NCO, second in command. Despite previous friction, he chose Burnanski as scout for his patrol savvy. He selected Joe Anderson for the B.A.R. he had proven adept at using, providing automatic weapon fire if needed. Wilcox thought to himself, *Wonder if the Lieutenant also picked Holy Joe because the kid will be praying for us all the way there and back. We're going to need it bad!*

Cooper, Nurnberg and Tobin remained behind. Troopers from the platoon's other squads would shift over and help them man the O.P. and cover the position above it on the ridge.

After midnight, the men gathered around the Lieutenant for a briefing and a quick bite to eat—three cold pancakes and half a ration can of "beef and pork loaf" apiece comprised the entire menu that could be scraped together. Everything washed down with a swig from their canteens.

"If it's any consolation to y'all," said the Lieutenant, "G-2 says the Krauts are short on rations too. Guess they gambled on easy success and made few plans about supplying in the field."

"Hey, guys! Something to wish you luck," Cooper said. He gave a piece of D-ration chocolate to each man, broken off the last bar he had squirreled away.

If it's to be my last meal, Wilcox thought with a smile, *at least it included chocolate.*

By the light of a hooded flashlight, the Lieutenant squatted, took a stick and began drawing a rough map in the snow. "Our current positions this side of the perimeter. Roads run along here, here and here. Railroad lines run over here. We'll skirt along the edge of the field past the farmhouse, turn into the woods and trek down along the creek. It's frozen now and covered with snow."

Like the rest of us, Wilcox thought.

The Lieutenant continued pointing with his stick. "It'll take us down through the forest over here to the north and east, by-pass some small farmsteads—possible enemy bivouacs—and bring us out at ridges rising just west of the sawmill around dawn. The closest ridge has a clearing near the top, overlooking the valley with the mill." He paused letting the men soak that in.

"So far, the brunt of Kraut attacks has been at our defenses down on the perimeter's southeast and southwest quadrants," the Lieutenant said. "We've held them so far. Division Intelligence gathered info from those Krauts y'all rounded up the other day, especially the map captured from that officer, tipping us off that they're hitting our area hard tomorrow or the next day." He smoothed out the snow with a gloved hand and drew again with his stick, scratching out an oval with squares and rectangles inside. "The valley with the sawmill is like this. Road runs along between the overlooking ridge and a belt of trees on the near side. Plenty of open land around the mill here, a large farmhouse over here, and out-buildings by the farmhouse and the mill. An obvious staging area for vehicles and places of shelter for men and supplies if they're mounting an attack in this sector." He paused again. "Here's where our patrol comes in: Our artillery's ammo's too precious now for blind interdiction barrages; we must scout the area and direct our artillery on an actual target. If we discover Krauts there in force, we call in the big guns."

Wilcox shifted his weight and thought, As *Coop would say, 'a lot of 'ifs!'*

"You may remember Engineer Sgt. Foley," the Lieutenant said. "He's volunteered to guide us."

"And bring trouble to the dirty scum who chased us out," Foley said. "Did some deer hunting around there before the breakthrough. I know the area well."

"And knows alternate routes in and out," the Lieutenant said. "We're bringing a few satchel charges along. If there's opportunity, we'll slip in with him, set charges and finish demolition cut short when the Krauts poured in, especially a store of explosives the engineers had in a building over here. But the main thing is directing the start of the artillery." He nodded at four Black artillerymen. One was the crusty sergeant who had come along the line earlier laying field telephone wire. "Sgt. Odom and his team will accompany us."

"We're running short on officer-observers, so you'll have to make do with me," the artilleryman said. "This is Corporal Steele, my radio man, and these are Privates Cave and Pollard, our escorts."

"Sgt. Wilcox and Privates Anderson, Friedenfeld, Vincenti, and Burnanski," the Lieutenant said, nodding at his men. "Odom's observer team's critical to the whole thing, so we must bring them safely there. They'll take position on high ground. If weather's clear and the Krauts are there in force, they'll start calling the artillery right away. If it's too foggy to see from the ridge, they'll wait in cover while we sneak down and scout the mill. As I said, Foley will set charges if the opportunity presents itself. Then we'll withdraw and protect Odom's team while they direct initial artillery fire." The Lieutenant stood. "The Krauts keep thinking we're licked, so we'll show 'em otherwise. Our goals are disrupting enemy activity and demonstrating our offensive power and fighting spirit."

"Once the party's started, we'll high-tail it out," Odom said.

"Any questions?"

"What if the Krauts 'start the party first,' and we get pinned down in the valley?" Vincenti asked.

"Odom's under strict orders to call in artillery if things get popping, whether we make it out or not," said the Lieutenant. "I'll send up a signal flare if I can."

"What if we run into an enemy patrol on the way in?" Friedenfeld asked.

"First, evade detection. Second, if we must deal with them, keep it quiet using knives and bayonets if possible. Third, open fire only on my order—I mean that for *everyone*, ONLY on my order! Non-airborne must trust my troopers to take care of the dirty work. We cannot give ourselves away heading in. Non-airborne are under orders to keep their safeties on unless hearing from me. If anything happens to me, Wilcox leads the way. If both of us fall, trust Burnanski to lead you through. He's chief scout and acting corporal for the patrol." Everyone's eyes swiveled toward Burnanski at this acknowledgment of his ability, but his hardened features remained impassive.

The patrol loaded up on ammo and grenades, both fragmentation and phosphorus, and fixed bayonets to rifles and carbines. They wrapped their helmets in white cloth, and everyone wore a white bed sheet, tied up poncho-style, as snow camouflage, with bandoliers, cartridge belts, side arms, and knives secured outside. Silence was paramount. The Lieutenant personally checked everyone and their gear one last time for telltale noises, a procedure foreign to the non-airborne element.

The Lieutenant headed the men out into the night. A light snow fell on them as they trudged along the edge of the forest past the remains of the Solvay's farm house, now a heap of blasted stones and blackened timbers from both sides' artillery and mortar fire. The snow shower grew heavy, a welcome thing now. It meant a rise in temperature, though still around freezing, and it screened their movement.

Past the farm, the Lieutenant sent Burnanski scouting ahead, leading the patrol through the trees down into the ravine, turning east and north along the creek bed. They crept beneath a bridge on the two-lane road beyond the farm, leery of possible observers up above. Off to their left, the way led across the fields and forests of the previous patrol. They trudged stiffly on, keeping weapons protected from the snow and watching for the enemy, wary of mines and other deadly *Sprengfallen*.

Burnanski led them past three of these traps as they skirted below a German *Biwak* on their right, a counterpart to the squad's encampment off to the west. He guided them around a place where the Germans came down to the creek and broke the ice for water. Hearing voices of the unseen enemy resting in their *Schützenlöchern* not far away increased tension to a razor's edge.

Burnanski halted the men. The Lieutenant signaled them into the trees on their left. A few minutes later, a three-man German patrol came down to the creek. Two boys and an older man turned and headed west on a path up the ravine.

"Ich wünschte, wir hätten die Straße Pflicht. Patrouillieren diesen Strom ist böse," complained one of the boys. "Es ist furchtbar kalt. Ich denke nicht, wird heraus Amerikaner heute Abend."

"Lassen Sie uns beeilen und beenden diese Patrouille. Ich bin hungrig. Mein Magen knurren," whined another.

"Ruhig, Jungs! Aufhören zu jammern! Achten Sie sorgfältig, oder Sie sich in einem unserer eigenen Minen laufen," said the older man. "Ich will nicht einen traurigen Brief schreiben und brechen Herzen deiner Mutter!"

The Germans continued on their way west. Burnanski crept along out of sight behind them, knife in hand, making sure they'd gone on. The Lieutenant held the others in place until Burnanski returned and signaled "all clear."

"What were they saying?" the Lieutenant whispered to Friedenfeld.

"One of the boys complained about being on patrol and the cold.

He thought no Americans would be out. The other whined about being hungry and his growling stomach. The old guy told 'em to quit jabbering and pay attention to their own mines or there'd be a sad letter home to momma."

"Old guy sounds like an NCO. Good thing the kids are making tracks out in front. The old guy might've noticed our own fresh tracks coming down."

Burnanski came back, gave an "Okay" sign, and the Lieutenant moved the men out of the trees and back on their way along the creek bed. Burnanski led them on again, watching for springs or other places with thin ice, twisting along the watercourse through the shrouded woods, then around three ridges. After they had gone another mile, the snow shower stopped.

Dawn approached and so did their objective, on schedule for a glimpse of the valley at first light. The Lieutenant, Foley and Burnanski had a brief whispered discussion before pressing on up the final ridge. The airborne element spread out. The artillerymen and engineer waited in the trees while the troopers secured the clearing and its perimeter. They found no traps or other signs of German activity.

"This is the 'picnic' spot I told you about," Foley whispered to the Lieutenant. "On a clear morning, you'd see the whole valley down below."

"Surprised the enemy doesn't have someone posted up here," said the Lieutenant.

"Perhaps a good sign for us," said Foley. "Letting down their guard through overconfidence."

"We won't make the same error."

The sun rose behind gray overcast, but because of warmer temperatures, a ground fog shrouded the valley floor under a sea of white. Only the dark tops of the tallest trees rose above.

"This is where we leave Odom and his team," the Lieutenant said.

"We're facing east. The mill's in a clearing within the bowl-shaped valley below," Foley said, drawing in the snow with his bayonet. "Trees surrounding the clearing on all sides, with an entrance road at the northwest corner, tree-covered ridges like this one all around. Road coming from the east along the north side, another coming in from the south along the foot of this ridge. Roads intersect by the entrance to the clearing." He gestured at toward the unseen valley trying to describe what lay down beneath the fog and continued tracing in the snow. "In the valley clearing, there's a large farmhouse about here and two barn-like sheds on the left. The sawmill itself is in a long open-sided shed on the right. When we pulled out, cut lumber lay in a dozen stacks here on this side of the mill shed. Uncut logs in big piles on the other side. Our general supply shed is between the stacked lumber and the tree line on this side. Way on the far right, by itself, is a smaller metal shed we used for storing demolition equipment and explosives. All the buildings were set to blow, but the Krauts probably cleared out the charges. At least that's what American engineers would do, and I know the Germans are thorough. They may have returned them to the demotions shed with the other explosives. All the more to blow, if we can set it off."

"Because of the fog, we'll have to slip down for a good look-see," the Lieutenant said. "Artillerymen, take your weapons off safety now. Be careful about opening fire on us when we return. We may be coming in a hurry."

"I'll see to it," Odom said.

"Watch for my red flare. You should see it go up above this soup. Krauts may send up flares of their own, trying to catch us, but red color signals Krauts assembling. Make your call, direct fire and skedaddle. Hopefully, we'll make it back and haul out with you, but don't wait on us if we're hung up below and take the alternate route back, just in case." He turned to his troopers. "From this point on, expect lots of Krauts: Patrols, sentries, maybe a defensive perimeter, possible mines. Traffic on the highway too. No voice above a whisper. Stay close. Single file. Step into the tracks of the man in front of you where you can. Burnanski, on point. B.A.R., up front with me. Wilcox, bring up the rear."

Without the falling snow to screen their movements, they advanced in cautious stages through the trees down toward the roadway. They each stepped into the footprints of the man in front to obscure their numbers from any patrol discovering their tracks in the snow. They paused under the cover of low brush beneath the trees when they arrived at the paved road below.

The bullet-ridden, twisted remains of an American 4×4 utility truck lay resting nose first in the deep ditch on the opposite side, a relic of the ill-fated retreat less than a week ago. Behind the smashed-in windshield, the frozen, snow-covered body of a dead G.I. slumped over the steering wheel.

"Poor Smitty," Foley whispered to himself.

Burnanski and the Lieutenant crept out to the highway, scouting each way, but saw and heard nothing in the fog. Burnanski squatted down and brushed the fresh snow away from the road surface, revealing packed, frozen tracks from previous days beneath, including the distinctive tread marks from armored vehicles. They saw other, smaller tracks, more recent —fresh Wehrmacht bootprints in the new fallen snow along the edge of the road. He whispered to the Lieutenant, "Jackboots headed north, maybe a security patrol, but no vehicles since the last snow."

The Lieutenant returned to the trees and whispered his instructions to the others, "We'll cross the road and check out the big area beyond the belt of trees. Brush out our tracks in case somebody comes along behind us." Taking a quick look both ways, he hurried his men across and past the corpse in the wrecked truck. Wilcox used a pine branch to blur signs of their crossing into the new snow.

The patrol entered the belt of trees and headed to their right. They paused by the inner edge of the forest, weapons ready, eyes scanning, our ears tuned to the slightest noise, aware of the enemy's proximity. The gray shapes of buildings loomed through the fog. Heavy smoke rose from a chimney on the largest, suspended over it in a thick layer held by the fog.

The Lieutenant held up his hand, gesturing, "Halt!"

They could hear German voices from the large farmhouse on the left. Occasional laughter sounded from within.

Burnanski's whisper to the Lieutenant was barely audible, "Enjoying their breakfast. Smell the wood smoke."

"Feasting on captured stores," the Lieutenant muttered, barely moving his lips.

"Cooks had a couple full-sized hams saved for Christmas," Foley whispered. "We unloaded almost a ton of potatoes and 10-in-1's the day before they ran us out."

The Lieutenant scanned the scene. "Couple half-tracks parked next to the house."

Burnanski pointed to the right. "More half-tracks and a pair of assault guns in a Laager by the large shed."

"Fuel dump near-by," muttered the Lieutenant.

Wilcox thought, *Assembling for an attack, as we feared!*

The Lieutenant soaked in the details for another minute.

124

Burnanski tugged on the Lieutenant's sleeve and pointed down at the snow by the inside edge of the forest to their left. The rest of them saw them too: Tracks of many hobnailed boots heading out to the forest and back. He whispered, "Coming out to the near patch of woods on the left as a latrine. Got to move away."

"Continue down to the right," Foley said. "Check out the demolitions shed."

The patrol moved around through the trees, away from the house, past the sawmill shed and parked vehicles. They came behind the lone demolitions shed, a small sheet metal-sided building with a corrugated metal roof. Several layers of sandbags stacked against the outer metal walls of the shed. Looking back through the fog toward their previous spot in the woods, they saw dim shapes walking out from the house toward the trees they had vacated. Other shapes now moved to and from the armored vehicles, the house and other buildings, but no movement toward or from the demolitions shed.

"Setting charges only in this shed," Foley explained. "Too many Krauts walking around near the others."

"Probably slept in them overnight," the Lieutenant said. "Vincenti, Burnanski, Creep in with Foley. Take out any guards. Keep it quiet."

Vincenti slipped on his brass knuckles. He pulled out his second-best stiletto, popped the spring blade out. Burnanski slipped his jump knife from its ankle sheath.

"Y'all have ten minutes, max," whispered the Lieutenant. "Then we pull out with or without you. We'll launch the flare and head southwest toward the railroad line if shooting starts over here, drawing them away from Odom up on the ridge."

Snow began falling again as the patrol watched Burnanski step out, followed by Vincenti and Foley with his satchel charges. The trio dashed across the open ground, keeping the shed between them and the Germans, buildings and vehicles in the fog farther north. The engineer crouched behind the shed, while Vincenti and Burnanski crept around either side to the front, checking for guards. They disappeared for a moment. Vincenti reappeared and gestured for Foley. He disappeared around the front of the shed as well. Wilcox and Joe kept watch for sentries on patrol during this operation. Tension grew each second with the men inside the shed. Four anxious minutes later, the trio came around the little building and ran back to the waiting patrol.

"No guards," Vincenti whispered. "Only a large, 'easy-open' padlock."

"Overconfidence plays again in our favor," the Lieutenant said.

"Krauts removed some, but still a quarter ton of TNT and C3 in there," Foley rapidly whispered. "I set charges in front and behind the stores. If the Krauts come along before it blows, they may only find the charge in front. I'm not sticking around to see if they do. Let's hustle."

Buddy, I'm with you! thought Wilcox.

"Moving back!" the Lieutenant whispered. They hurried through the dense trees near where they had crossed the road. Emerging from the forest a dozen yards beyond the rear of the wrecked utility truck, the Lieutenant shot up his hand, bringing them to a halt. He directed the men back into the cover of the trees. The ground vibrated with the rumble of engines as a convoy of heavy vehicles approached from the south, cutting them off from the ridge on the far side of the road. Crouching in the woods, they watched as four Wehrmacht M.P.'s riding *Kettenkrader* light tractors and then two Nebelwerfer, half-track-mounted rocket launchers— the dreaded "Screaming Mimi's"—roll by. Two of the M.P.'s dismounted and directed the half-tracks into the clearing by the farmhouse. Self-propelled artillery and half-track infantry vehicles rumbled along behind them at wide intervals and a slow pace because of snow and ice on the roadway. Each vehicle joined the others assembling by the farmhouse.

The Lieutenant huddled the patrol together so they could hear him above the vehicle noise. "Part of a Panzer unit," the Lieutenant said. "This could go on for a while. How much longer before those charges go?"

Foley checked his watch and said, "Thirteen minutes. This is still kinda close when that amount of TNT and C-3 blows."

I'll say, thought Wilcox.

"Have to chance it in the snow between vehicles," the Lieutenant said. "I'll go across first with Wilcox covering and signal for you. Foley and then Vincenti and Friedenfeld, then Anderson and Burnanski bringing up the rear."

Joe nodded, and Burnanski grunted assent.

Another vehicle passed and faded into the falling snow. The Lieutenant leaped the deep ditch and dashed across, followed closely by Wilcox. Wilcox turned and hurried along the trees heading down to the left. He began signaling to the Lieutenant whenever there a gap appeared in the stream of vehicles. The Lieutenant judged the intervals between groups of vehicles and directed the other men to dash across two at a time. It reminded Wilcox of when he had played elaborate neighborhood games of hide and seek with friends years before. Back then, he'd be watching for an opportunity when the one who was "it" stepped away, and signaled for his friends to run in from hiding, tag the goal and shout "free!" before "it" could catch them. *Only this time the one that's "it" is armed and ready to kill*, he thought.

Mercifully, the snowfall had increased, screening their crossing even more. Two more German vehicles passed slowly. Foley crossed the ditch and ran across into the forest on the other side. Another four vehicles felt their way through the falling snow. Vincenti and Friedenfeld each hurried across in turn. Only Anderson and Burnanski remained on the far side of the road.

Just before Joe's turn, Burnanski turned and whispered harshly in his ear, "Don't forget to pray, kid!"

Anderson, not taking his eyes off the Lieutenant, barely visible across the road, whispered back, "I am, and I'm praying for you too."

A deeper rumbling could be heard and felt through the frozen ground beneath the snow, coming nearer and nearer. The Lieutenant signaled, and Joe scrambled across the road. Before he was across, the Lieutenant signaled again, and Burnanski began his move. He cleared the ditch, but lost his footing on hidden ice and tumbled backward into the snowy ditch. He climbed out and began crossing the road. A massive Panther tank rumbled into view. Six snow smock-clad *SS-Panzergrenadiere*, armored infantrymen, clung to the tank's hull. Above on the turret, an officer in black SS uniform stood upright in the open command hatch screaming orders. His guttural voice shouted, and machine gun fire streamed past Burnanski. Burnanski froze as the bullets zipped by in front of him, tearing up a cloud of snow and chunks of frozen road. The infantry leaped from the hull and tumbled onto the snowy road. Some slipped and fell. Others brought their weapons up to fire.

Joe Anderson pivoted and shouted, "Ski, get down!" Bursting back across, he knocked Burnanski down in the road, both of their weapons flying away. A split second later, the tank's machine gun sprayed the road where Burnanski had stood, kicking up another cloud of snow and more chunks of frozen road. The Panzergrenadiere behind the tank opened erratic fire around the giant steel machine.

Bullets zinging past, Burnanski and Anderson rolled off into the ditch. They crawled down the ditch toward the wrecked truck. They squeezed into a small space beneath the wreck. The under-chassis tugged at their uniforms as they wormed through. The pair emerged behind the momentary cover the wreck offered. The officer standing in the tank hatch screamed for the Panzergrenadiere to attack. Bullets snapped around Burnanski and Anderson. Ricochets whined off the truck's carcass.

A sharp command from the Lieutenant, and the unseen patrol members across the road opened fire from the shelter of the woods. His red signal flare streaked up through the fog into the clear air above the scene. The patrol hit two of the Panzergrenadiere. The rest dropped into the ditch or crouched alongside the bulky tank, returning fire.

Burnanski nudged Anderson. "Artillery's coming! Do as I do." He grabbed a phosphorus grenade. You frag and me "Willie Pete." First two onto the tank, underhand, like bucket-toss at a carnival. Second pair over into the troops. Two and another two," he said, rushing the words even as he was pulling the pin from a "Willie Pete," white phosphorus grenade. Joe readied his fragmentation grenades.

Burnanski peered cautiously around the truck. Bullets whined near his head. "When I say, release safeties, count two and toss around this truck onto the tank. Lob the next pair right after. Run back across as soon as the next two pop. Release, one, two . . . NOW!"

The two leaned around either side of the wreck, lobbing their grenades in short arcs onto the deck at the front of the approaching tank. Without pause, they pulled pins and tossed grenades again.

CRACK! Shrapnel splinters from the first fragmentation grenade injured the tank's driver through his open hatch. The Panther jerked and swerved toward the ditch, dropping the standing officer into the turret cage. The "Willie Pete" rolled across the front deck and exploded a split-second later, showering burning particles around the front of the tank and through the open command cupola on top of the fallen officer. Pearlescent coiling tendrils of smoke from the burning phosphorus engulfed the tank, obscuring the driver and gunner's view.

The second pair of grenades flew over the tank, dropping among the infantrymen as the first pair exploded. The Panzergrenadiere scattered to avoid the grenades and grinding treads of the erratic tank. Another sharp explosion, the second fragmentation grenade, followed by a softer pop from the other 'Willie Pete.' A billowing cloud of smoke screened Burnanski and Joe's dash across. From the heavy pall came a crunch of twisted metal as the tank continued crawling forward, onto the back of the ruined truck. The truck collapsed beneath the behemoth machine. One of the tank's treads slid off the compacted wreckage, sending the forty-four ton monster lurching down at an angle onto a helpless Panzergrenadiere crouching in the ditch, cutting his pitiful scream of terror short.

Anderson and Burnanski sprinted out of the smoke cloud into the far tree line, while the patrol gave covering fire into the smoke. The Lieutenant withdrew the patrol up the ridge. The surviving Panzergrenadiere emerged from the smoke cloud. They ran across the road and spread out at the forest's edge behind the retreating paratroopers. Shots rang out. Joe stumbled and fell. He staggered up again and struggled up the ridge, grabbing the outside of his upper right leg, leaving a red trail in the snow.

Wilcox dropped to the rear, emptying his submachine gun in short bursts down at the Germans, shouting, "Get moving! Get moving!" Bullets zipped by. The tank shifted gears, backing up out of the ditch as the smoke thinned. The Panther reached level ground again. Wilcox's pulse raced as he heard the whir of its turret's electric motor traversing the 75mm main gun in his direction. *Get moving, yourself!*

Burnanski ran back down. Bullets tugged at his collar and left sleeve, ripping through the fabric but missing his neck and arm. He reached out, grabbed Joe by his ammo belt, and gave him support as the pair continued uphill. More bullets clipped branches and splattered into tree trunks over their heads.

The whine of the traversing of the turret stopped. The Lieutenant, listening for that moment, shouted, "Hit the dirt!" The patrol dropped to the ground. A round of high explosive ripped by and struck off to their left. The ground beneath them heaved at the blast. Their ears rang. Splinters, branches, snow and frozen clods of dirt cascaded all over them, but they ran on again before the debris settled.

Behind them whistles sounded. More vehicles carrying Greman infantry arrived, deployed and began an organized advance from the road up into the lower forest. Trees cracked, snapped and crashed as the growling Panther plowed its nose into the woods seeking for another clear shot at them.

Wilcox tossed two more smoke grenades down the ridge, obscuring the retreating patrol from view. Burnanski half carried, half-supported Joe, slipping and dodging up through the snowy trees.

A brilliant blue-white flash penetrated fog and snow, illuminating everything for a stark instant. A colossal blast wave swept knocked both

Germans and Americans to the ground. Trees swayed as the shock of the blast struck them. A great thunderclap of explosion roared from the valley. Broken branches, pine cones and snow showered down on everything and everyone. Echoes resounded from the surrounding ridges with angry rumbling.

"Fire in the hole!" Foley cried, barely heard above the din. "There she goes!"

Sounds ripped through the sky above, followed by less dramatic explosions down in the valley. Rain after the thunder, the American artillery barrage had begun.

And here it comes, thought Wilcox.

Anderson struggled back to his feet. Blood streamed down his right leg above the knee.

"Joe, you okay?" Burnanski asked

Joe spoke through clenched teeth, "Took one along my thigh. Hurts awful bad."

Burnanski pulled Joe behind a large tree and squatted for a quick inspection of his leg wound. Wilcox crouched beside them on one knee, firing short bursts downhill into the smoke and confusion below. Friedenfeld dropped behind a tree close by, firing down as well. Burnanski doffed his helmet and jerked off the towel he had draped over his head for warmth. With a yank, he ripped it in two. He folded one of the strips, placed it as a bandage directly over the bloody gash and tied the other strip around Joe's upper leg, holding the bandage in place.

"You do that pretty good," Joe said through clenched teeth as Burnanski finished tying the strips in place.

"Nothing like being shot at to get the adrenaline up," Burnanski grinned back at Joe, the first time Joe Anderson had ever seen Burnanski with a friendly grin. "All we can do for now," Burnanski said. He stood up, tapped Wilcox on the shoulder, put his arm around Joe, and grabbed his belt again. Together with Wilcox and Friedenfeld covering, they hurried up the rest of the ridge. A moment later, they tumbled to the ground, knocked down by the blast of a final round of high explosive from the tank obliterating the tree they had paused behind only moments before. They pulled themselves up and continued uphill.

The patrol reached the open crest of the ridge. They fanned out and fired briefly back down at the Germans to dissuade any from rushing up after them. Sgt. Odom gave final coordinates over the radio, temporarily directing artillery and smoke onto the road and the forward slope of the hill, covering their retreat.

The patrol cleared out, hurrying headlong down the reverse slope of the ridge. Behind them a billowing black cloud from burning fuel rose into gray morning sky. Friedenfeld took point this time as Burnanski continued to support and carry Joe along. Artillery rained down close behind them on the far slope.

The sounds of pursuit and the artillery barrage faded into the falling snow and ended three minutes later. The patrol rushed on back. They descended into the ravine, slipping and stumbling across the rocky creek bed and up the other side. They couldn't return the same they way they came, for fear of ambush, but followed along a field at the forest edge, heading west.

When they came near the farm with the German *Biwak* above the creek, Burnanski led them in skirting it along the tree line on the far side. Shots rang out from across the farm. Whistles sounded. A skirmish line formed and began a cautious advance across the fields behind them. Pushing on rather than returning fire, the Lieutenant directed the patrol into the bordering forest. A spent slug glanced off the back of Wilcox's helmet and sent it flying. He scooped up the headgear and put it back on without breaking a stride.

The patrol pressed on without a cleared path, tripping over snow-covered rocks and hidden roots, crashing through small thickets. Low branches lashed them in their haste. Thorns ripped their outer clothing and scratched exposed flesh.

They continued on, emerging from the forest and crossing the road east of the Solvay farm. Scattered gunfire sounded from the forest behind them. Bullets whined overhead and ricocheted off rubble as they hurried passed the shattered Solvay farmhouse. Friedenfeld sprinted on ahead, warning of their approach. The rest hurried behind until entering their lines at last.

The Lieutenant crawled over the stone wall, dropping beside Cooper and Nurnberg in the O.P. He grabbed the field telephone. The rest of the men dropped into the slit trench, breathing hard and watching him. His breath streaming out in clouds, he gave a call for the company mortars in range to fire on the pursuers. The resulting barrage was brief but satisfying.

Nurnberg manned the machine gun. "Sir, should I fire some bursts toward the farmhouse?"

"No. Might draw their mortars back on us," the Lieutenant said. "I think our own have run them off them for now. Thanks for asking. Keep an ear out for vehicles. If they do attack over here, they'll probably bring armored support."

"Enough adventure for one morning, eh?" said Cooper to Wilcox, popping in another hand-whittled toothpick.

Wilcox removed his helmet and showed him the dent. "Enough for the rest of my life."

"Thank you, troopers," Sgt. Odom said, "for bringing us safely there and back."

"Same here," said Foley.

"Our pleasure," said Wilcox.

"But can't say we should to do it again anytime soon," said Vincenti.

The artillerymen and Sgt. Foley moved up over the ridge back toward their respective units. The rest of the patrol headed for their foxholes. The Lieutenant paused beside Burnanski, who was applying more first aid to Joe's wound. "Good job today, Burnanski! We'll get Anderson off to the aid station soon as you finish up."

"All right, sir."

The Lieutenant moved off. Burnanski applied sulfa from his kit and wrapped a regular field dressing on Joe's right thigh. He leaned close to Joe and a low voice asked, "Crazy kid, why'd you save my life?"

Anderson smiled and winced from the pain in his leg. "I'd do that for any of my friends."

Burnanski frowned and whispered. "How can I be your friend? I've treated you worse than dirt. You must think that I'm such a sinner."

"No, I've been trying to love you the same way my Lord Jesus Christ does. He was called 'the friend of sinners.'"

Burnanski stared at Joe for a moment and said, "Once had a friend die for me. It still haunts me. Sometimes I can just scream from the regret. I froze out on that road today because the whole thing came rushin' back to me. I don't know your Christ this way, not the way you're talking' about."

Joe said simply, "He knows all about you. He died for you on the cross."

Burnanski scowled and turned away. "I'm rotten. Wicked. Headed for a 'Christless eternity,' same as those dead Germans you talked about the other day."

Joe looked up at Burnanski, keeping his gaze steady. "People who know they're sinners are the very ones Christ receives. He rejects those who think they aren't. We're all sinners deserving Hell, but the blood of Jesus Christ will cleanse anyone from their sin."

Burnanski began wrapping a clean field dressing around the wound. "What about my drinking, fighting, cussing, gambling?"

"Jesus took the punishment for all of those. Jesus cares about you, will transform you deep within, and give you victory over all the root problems those outward sins sprout from."

"I want a break from the past, but I've gone so far in sinning. I've tried changing. It didn't work."

"That's why we need a Savior. Can't do it ourselves. When my dad died, I turned bitter. I moped around. Acted brutally mean to my sister. Bullied kids. Got into fights at school. Almost expelled."

"You? Sounds more like me." Burnanski pulled ends of the bandage tight and tied them. "Hard to believe you'd be that way."

"I was, but when I received Christ, He changed me and gave me victory over it."

Burnanski packed up the remains of his first aid kit. "Would he do that for me?"

"If you'll believe on Jesus Christ, He'll change your life too. You'll be born again, spiritually, born from above with a new nature responding to God. Be whiter in your soul than this snow around us and have a new beginning."

"A new beginning . . ." Burnanski said. "Have to think on that."

"After salvation, I had the in-dwelling Holy Spirit and the Word of God to help me find victory in Christ. You can find victory in Jesus Christ too."

Stretcher-bearers from the aid station arrived as Burnanski finished up. "Not so sure about that, Joe." He helped the bearers ease Anderson onto their stretcher.

As the men lifted Joe from the ground, he reached out, grabbing Burnanski's sleeve, pulling him close and saying in his ear, "Ski, it's in God's word, and He doesn't lie."

The other men in the squad rested in their foxholes, recovering from the exertion and shock of the patrol and wondering over the shock of unexpected dialog now opening between Burnanski and Joe Anderson.

Strange and eventful day, thought Wilcox. *Up 'til now D-Day took the cake, but this one's stranger still!*

* * * * * *

GREIER

"Furious" would be a mild term describing Sturmbannführer Greier's mood the rest of the day. His headquarters area lay in shambles. *Vehicles destroyed and damaged. Supplies lost. Men dead, wounded, shaken in spirit. Precious petrol gone up in smoke!* The worst part: The devastating attack he personally planned no longer possible! *Kaputt!*

Not only had a small band of saboteur *Fallschirmjäger* infiltrated his assembly area and brought on this havoc, but two of the impudent foes also hurled grenades at his personal tank! He thought, *If the great blast preceding the artillery barrage hadn't killed the Volksgrenadier officer in charge of area security, I'd have shot the Dummkopf myself!*

The attack injured Greier himself. His left shoulder dislocated while falling into the command tank, his arm now in a sling. His right hand and forearm bandaged where searing phosphorus particles burned through his glove and clothing deep into his flesh. He ran the exposed finger tips of his right hand gingerly up over another bandage, this one covering a tender, aching lump on the back of his head. The side of his skull glanced off the hatch coaming as he fell into the turret when the grenades exploded. The pain inside his head throbbed worse than the wound outside.

"A concussion as well as a contusion," the *Mediziner* who treated his wounds had said. "Best to take it easy for a few days. Rest your other wounds as well." *Talking to me in a patronizing tone, as if I were a doddering pensioner at a spa!*

"Idiot!" growled Greier at the time. "I don't have a few days!"

I would've punched through their lines this afternoon and dined in Bastogne city-hall this evening!

Growing doubt flickered through his mind. *Perhaps the Führer had bitten off too much. Perhaps we will fail short of our goal, lose to these inferiors. What will happen to me then? Imprisonment? War crimes tribunal?* He shook the uncertainty from his thoughts. *Never! Absolute trust! Absolute devotion to the Supreme Will! Deutschland über alles!*

Greier yelled for his surviving aide. "Summon all *Kompanie* commanders! A meeting in fifteen minutes for damage assessment, regrouping and attack. And get *Korps* artillery on the radio!"

In the meantime . . . I'll gather my forces, goad that Volksgrenadier Division into action and teach these 'Adlerkopf' Fallschirmjäger a lesson in death history won't forget!

CHAPTER THIRTEEN

East of Bastogne

December 22, 1944

As Allied defenses stiffened along both shoulders and west of the Bulge, the German drive toward Antwerp began to stall. Hitler impatiently glared at his map showing the Americans still holding out at Bastogne. Critical forward momentum of his massive operation slipped away every moment he did not possess those roads. Nothing must blunt his offensive. He stomped his feet, pounded the map and demanded Bastogne. His kowtowing generals assured him that he would have the city as a Christmas present.

* * * * * * *

WILCOX

Journal entry for Friday, December 22nd:

Wonder how much longer we'll be able to hold out. Kraut artillery pounded us all day long. Guess yesterday's patrol stirred their wrath. A major enemy push on the southern perimeter, and all kinds of activity elsewhere testing and taxing our defenses. In the afternoon, the Germans launched a battalion-sized attack directly through the forest at a road junction in the sector to our left, hard-pressing the troopers manning the roadblock over there. Most of our company headed to the rescue,l swinging out into the woods. We hit the Krauts on their left flank. Tank destroyers hurried out from town and held off assault guns and a Panther tank approaching from the north. We joined up with the other company and drove the German infantry off. They left their supporting tanks exposed, and the beasts had to withdraw.

We pursued some of the Krauts back through the woods. Most of the time, we couldn't see anything much to shoot at, but once we drew close enough to get into a grenade fight with them, lobbing a few volleys back and forth in the thick undergrowth beneath the trees. If only we were kids throwing harmless snowballs!

The attack depleted our pitiful reserves, killing my old friend, Sgt. Avery, and three other guys from the next platoon, wounding a dozen more. We lost five men from our already weakened platoon, including Tobin, one of my squad's replacements. Mortar got him. If he survives surgery in our make-shift field hospital, he won't be playing baseball anymore, unless they start a league for one-legged players. With him and Anderson gone, this squad is down to only six men.

Our supplies are dwindling out. Not much food to go around. Our ammo situation is past critical. We've only got three rounds left for the platoon's last working mortar and one full belt of ammo split between the squad's two machine guns. Nothing for the bazooka. We pooled the remaining rifle ammo, which came out to about half a bandoleer per man. We hear the big artillery's almost out of ammo as well.

"Discouraged" doesn't seem adequate to describe the men. It's easy to cave-in to hopelessness and despair when there's no change from day to day for the better, only for the worse. We're too cold, too hungry, and we've too little time left. Tempers flare and apathy is taking over; some guys have had all they can endure. It's tempting to envy those with wounds taking them away from the line. The dead look so peaceful—their suffering is over at last. If only something would restore our hope.

That evening Joe Anderson limped out to their position.

Cooper's handcrafted toothpick fell out when he saw him. "You should be lyin' around resting that leg wound, kid."

Anderson simply said. "We're short of men, so this evening the general's ordered remaining clerks, cooks, and the walking wounded out to the line. I can limp around, so I came back to be with my friends." He looked directly at Burnanski on that final word. Burnanski frowned and turned away.

"Good to have you home, my boy," said Wilcox.

"Saw Tobin in a basement back in town," Joe said. "Tough about losing his foot like that. Spent the afternoon with him. They're doing what they can for him, considering the lack of doctors and supplies. He misses you guys and says thanks for putting up with him."

"Glad you could see him," Wilcox said. "Burnanski and Cooper, your turn in the O.P."

Cooper whined, "Aw, Mom, I got a cold!"

"Good! Everybody else has pneumonia!" Wilcox shot back.

Anderson spoke up, "Let me take Coop's place. Except for my hike out here, I've just been sitting around all day."

Wilcox examined him for a second, gauging this strange young man who wanted to share a frozen hole for two hours with the guy who had recently seemed to be his sworn enemy. "All right," he said, "if you think you can handle it. Cooper can go with Nurnberg next shift."

"Thanks, Joe," said Cooper.

Joe Anderson and Burnanski moved down through the trees to the new observation post, Joe hobbling along on his sore leg and 'Ski giving him support over fallen trees and rough patches. They relieved Friedenfeld and Vincenti. The pair, cheered by Joe's return, handed off field-glasses, telephone and machine gun and shuffled stiffly back up to warm themselves at the aid station.

Joe and 'Ski sat together in silence for a long time gazing out at the road and beyond to the ruined farm as a light snow fell on them.

Finally, 'Ski spoke quietly, so quietly Joe could barely hear him, "The division's fought through some tough scrapes, but this is the toughest. Don't know if we'll hold out much longer. Everyone seems to be giving up. Time has about run out. I don't know if God is for real as you say, but if you've ever prayed, pray now for God to do something so that I might know what you say is true. I'll keep watch."

Joe Anderson bowed his head and began to pray aloud softly, "Dear Lord, I thank You that You love us and care for us more than we know. You know how little we have left to fight with. We need food and ammunition. We're worn out from the tension and the cold. Wounded pile up in basements all over town. The remaining medical staff has no anesthetics and is short of other supplies."

He paused, swallowed and continued, "The hope of many soldiers is fading, our strength slips away. But You are the Creator of the clouds and the snow. You are the Mighty God who answered Elijah's prayer and sent the rain on Israel. You stilled the wind and the waves out on Galilee. You are greater than this weather and more powerful than Hitler and all his army.

"O, my God, that the truth of the gospel may be shown to my fellow soldiers, especially to my friend 'Ski, clear these skies that the planes may bring us aid."

'Ski kept a lookout, and Joe continued praying silently. The snowfall decreased. A short time later, it petered out and stopped all. 'Ski turned to Joe, patted his arm, and pointed at the snow-less sky.

Joe nodded back and whispered, "Praise the Lord."

The pair returned from the observation post. The night grew bitterly cold. No one in the squad could sleep. They endured the dropping temperatures, shivering, massaging their feet, and beating their arms across their chests, weary of winter and of war.

Ice crystals began forming on every exposed surface, adding to their misery and labors. They struggled with numb fingers to wipe the white rime from weapons to keep them from freezing up.

'Ski shared his foxhole with Joe the rest of that night. Joe continued to pray. In the wee hours of the morning, Burnanski pushed aside the pine boughs covering the hole and peeked out. Something different in the night. He poked his whole head out, then suddenly stood and began to shout excitedly, "Hey, I see a star! More stars! The sky is clearing! The sky is clearing!"

At first, some of the men in their miserable stupor thought he warned of an attack. Then they realized what Burnanski shouted. They emerged stiffly from their frozen holes and gazed at the sky and at Anderson in wonder.

Anderson, a tear streaming down his cheek, gazed up into the cloudless sky, and began to sing softly, "Praise God from whom all blessings flow . . ."

First one voice, and then another picked up the words and the volume, "Praise Him all creatures here below . . ."

Burnanski surprised everyone, joining them with a passable baritone, "Praise Him above ye heavenly host . . ."

The quintet on the ridge sang, "Praise Father, Son, and Holy Ghost," joined in by the duo down in the O.P.

The septet even sang an "Amen" with a fair attempt at harmony.

"All right, that's enough!" Wilcox said. "Get back down. Keep quiet before Reynolds comes over and chews us all out for that racket!"

* * * * * * *

GROSSHOLTZ

Out on patrol, equally sleepless German survivors from the previous day's attack crept through the forest. Their mission dragged on much longer than anticipated. The night grew frigid under a clearing sky. The Landsers trudged snow. They toiled against frost build-up on their weapons and wanted to quit, but knowing the fury of their enraged commanders, Oberfeldwebel Grossholtz goaded his men and boys on. The Volksgrenadier couldn't return to the shelter of their Biwak without achieving their objective: Determining the position of the enemy Widerstandslinie, the line of resistance, in this sector.

Grossholtz edged his men and boys along, parallel to the route the withdrawing *Alderkopf Fallschirmjäger*, "Eagle-Head" paratroopers, followed after their raid and after their counter-attack through these woods the other day. His Landsers had not dared penetrate this far west before. Apprehension among the boys and men increased with every step. They probed on and on, reaching a spot where the forest thinned along a roadway running north and south at the base of a long ridge.

Keeping his men screened within the forest, Grossholtz turned them south, skirting the road. A faint noise rose in the night, out of place in the frosty woodland. The wary Feldwebel halted his Landsers and the scuffle of their boots through the snowy bracken. Alert to danger, he inched forward alone, past his own point-men until he came near an ice-bound creek passing beneath the road and descending into a ravine heading north.

His men crouched behind him, weapons ready, waiting his signal. Grossholtz strained his ears, seeking to identity the alien sound. *Was it animal? Vehicular? Human activity? Near at hand?* Aware that noises carry further in the dry air of a frigid night, he held his breath, lest even that obscure other sounds. *There!* He caught the noise again. Past the creek and the road, beyond the ridge to his right, *Voices. A group of voices . . . singing!* He recognized the tune as one his church sang with words from the hymn "Herr Gott, dich loben alle wir," meaning "Lord God, We Praise Thee All."

Of all things, Amerikaner singing a hymn of praise beneath the star-filled sky? Grossholtz marveled at these strange *Adlerkopf* who fought like devils and yet sang church hymns. *A bad omen, it seems. My boys and men have suffered enough at their hands. This patrol's mission is accomplished, as far as I'm concerned!*

He marked his map. He turned his Landsers around, hurrying them away into the safer depths of the frozen woods.

CHAPTER FOURTEEN

Outside Bastogne

December 24, 1944

Wilcox

Journal entry for late Sunday evening, December 24th:

It's Christmas Eve, and the weather has finally cleared! We've received some resupply, but the bulk of it was artillery shells, so we're running short on small arms ammo and rations again. A small surgical team came in by glider, set up in a garage and has their hands full and then some with all the wounded needing treatment. God bless those brave doctors and nurses!

Heavy German attack all day—tanks and self-propelled guns making big trouble. Plenty of their infantry too, but not as aggressive.

When things died down, we fell back to another position in the woods. Our commanders wanted to draw more enemy armor out into the open, move troopers away from that danger and let our air support cover the roads for us. We just don't have the ammo in our sector to deal with armor directly for the time being.

Our commander sent a "Merry Christmas" greeting to the troops. Imagine, getting a Christmas card in the middle of all this mess! Just a piece of printed cardboard, but it made everybody smile. Part of it said, "'What's merry about this?' you ask. Just this: We have stopped cold everything that's been thrown at us from the North, East, South, and West. The Germans surround us; their radios blare our doom. Their commander demanded from me 'an honorable surrender to save the U.S. troops from total annihilation.' He received the following official reply: 'To the German Commander: "NUTS!" Signed: The American Commander.'"

After rejecting this ultimatum, our commander ordered some units out on a limited counterattack showing the Krauts that we mean to fight it out. We made that long-range patrol mission a couple days ago, so our company stayed back in reserve.

Today word spread about Allied radio news reports saying that Patton's Third Army is trying to break through to us from the south but having a slow go of it. Hope they get here before our company's cluster of shallow graves back in the woods grows any larger.

Because of our planes patrolling the skies during the day, we fear possible night attacks, but the only trouble we heard after dark was German planes bombing the heart of Bastogne, no doubt in retaliation for our general's defiant reply. What a contrast with the spirit of Christmas! We do have some magnanimity on the American side of things —heard that our commander gave some Belgian nurses permission to sing "Silent Night" to German prisoners of war we've locked up in the city jail.

I write this by hooded flashlight, hunkered down in the observation post next to Cooper. Being Christmas Eve, the company's non-com's are keeping watch in the O.P.'s all night and letting our weary men sleep in as a Christmas present. Heaven knows they need it. Speaking of heaven, even as this battle continues, I can't help thinking of the first Christmas long ago, a wonder of that penetrates even the horror of this war. The stars shine brightly above us in this dry air, like Bethlehem's star from ages past.

* * * * * * *

Help from the south slogged its way north toward Bastogne, but the German forces fought furiously, keeping it from breaking through even as they still sought to crush the city's beleaguered defenders. Hope that rose with the airdrop faded when the adrenaline wore off and the tenuous reality of the situation returned. The desperate needs of the defenders could not be met by airdrop alone. Hammered in their thin lines, the Bastogne defenders continued growing weaker and weaker.

* * * * * * *

The Andersons

Candles lit the Sunday evening service in honor of it being Christmas Eve, a tradition going back to the little suburban church's founding. The only electric lights adorned a Christmas tree in one corner of the platform and illuminated an American flag in the other.

The volunteer music director led the congregation in singing "O Holy Night." Mrs. Anderson and Susan stood together in a pew three rows back, sharing a hymnal in the flickering light. Susan trembled, thinking of Joe's desire to serve Christ in the war, as she sang, "Truly He taught us to love one another; His law is love and His gospel is peace; Chains shall He break for the slave is our brother; And in His name all oppression shall cease . . . ."

Mrs. Anderson put her arm around her daughter and gave her a reassuring squeeze. They both knew Joe loved this particular service and missed him much. *Was it so long ago?* she pondered. *Joe standing up in front of the church dressed in his daddy's old bathrobe playing the part of the Inn Keeper, and Susan wearing cardboard wings as one of the angels in the annual Christmas Pantomime. Both kids have grown. An evil shadow falls upon the world. Dear Lord Jesus, help Joe to shine Your light in the darkness.*

* * * * * * *

The winter sun rose on the squad's sector of the position away from the road. Others from the squad manned the new O.P. or transferred scattered supplies found in the woods. Having been on watch all night, Wilcox sat exhausted on the edge of his current foxhole mulling over the events of the past week. In the past, he would have dismissed his melancholy line of thinking that morning, but fatigue, cold, constant stress and lack of food had assaulted his reserves of energy and resolve, besides the physical combat he'd endured. *We're hanging on by a thread growing thinner and thinner as time slips away,* he thought. *The whole perimeter will collapse if the Krauts penetrate its flimsy shell. Is it worth the constant effort, the precious lives it takes holding out? Maybe it's inevitable the Germans will crush us. Maybe it'd be better to accept the surrender they offer than be maimed or blown to bits for nothing!*

He heard a low murmur. It wasn't from Cooper, who dozed in a foxhole near-by. Wilcox crawled after the sound trying to identify its source and found it: Joe Anderson praying alone down in the farthest foxhole. Too lame to carry supplies, he'd remained behind.

Wilcox heard him pray, "Dear Lord, send relief soon. The guys have little spirit left to fight. Keep them safe and give them the will to live, so that they may come to know the truth of the gospel. Help me to show them the love of Christ. In eternity, it won't matter if we win this battle against the Germans if the battle for men's souls is lost. Some seem close to salvation. Protect them so they might trust in You. I pray especially for 'Ski. Help me continue answering his questions and demonstrating Your love. Help him to understand Your forgiveness. Oh, God! Do whatever it takes! My life if necessary, if that'll bring him and the other guys to salvation."

Wilcox, embarrassed for eavesdropping on something so personal, crept away in case Joe looked out and noticed him listening. He sat down on the edge of his foxhole again and returned to his meditation with even more food for thought.

CHAPTER FIFTEEN

East of Bastogne

December 25, 1944

Wilcox

Journal entry for Monday, December 25th:

Merry Christmas! An army chaplain came along the line early this morning presenting our official 1944 G.I. Christmas presents: A new pair of socks for each of us. It wasn't the trip to Paris I'd been hoping for, but as they say, "It's the thought that counts!" I pulled off the old, unwashed ones, put on the new and pulled the old ones back on over those. Slightly warmer feet, courtesy of Uncle Sam!

The Germans celebrated Christmas Day by attacking again, mostly from the north. From the whine of diving aircraft overheard and explosions we heard over the ridge, evidently our planes hit some Krauts by our old bivouac overlooking the Solvay farm. Good thing we moved back. Our air support stopped them, and some ground units counterattacked even though we're running low on food and ammo again. Everyone's dead tired and hunger gnaws within, but now that the planes drove the Krauts off, we're heading out soon, taking up whatever's left of our original position.

* * * * * * *

Burnanski

The platoon moved slowly through the battle-damaged forest and split up by squads. Wilcox led his handful of men back to their old foxholes along what once was a wooded ridge. Minds felt as numb as their bodies from the cold, malnutrition and fatigue. The possibility of coming upon Germans or their booby-traps forced weary troopers awake.

The area lost its familiarity, filled with a strange silence, putting everyone on edge. German *Panzergrenadier* swept up the unoccupied ridge the day before, tossing grenades and spraying everything with submachine gun fire. Their fruitless attack altered the terrain. Makeshift roofs over the old fox holes were caved in or blown away. The returning American troopers found makeshift roofs over their old holes caved in or blown away. The holes now filled with snow and debris. Fallen timber, branches and frozen clods of soil littered the surrounding ground. The attack stripped away most of the rest of the forest canopy. Remaining trees looked even more scarred and shredded from gunfire and artillery than the men remembered. Hobnail boot prints marked the snow and soil everywhere.

Wilcox surveyed the devastated woodland. "Well, Coop, no need to whittle any more toothpicks for a long, long while. Krauts whittled plenty for ya."

Cooper picked up a splinter. Stuck it in his mouth. Rolled it around with his tongue. Spat it out again. "Not the same," the toothpick *connoisseur* said. "Mass production's no substitute for hand-craftsmanship."

The squad worked their way down hill through the stumps and fallen tree trunks to the edge of the road. They sensed that the Lieutenant had his reservations about returning, uneasy about moving his men back into places that might now be booby-trapped or set up for an ambush. After sundown, he would send patrols out to sweep the area north, east and south. For the time being, the men scanned the fields and forest across the road but detected no enemy presence. Everything seemed all right, but their uneasiness persisted.

The intersection of the road with the farm lane bore obvious witness to enemy assault and allied air support dealing with deadly force upon exposed German armor. The charred hulk of a *Sturmgeschütz* assault gun sprawled where Cooper and Burnanski had laid their mines days before. Treads blown off one side by a mine, the disabled armored vehicle had fallen prey to an Allied fighter-bomber and caught fire. "Brewing up," as the British say, the fire set-off the assault gun's ammunition. The explosion ripped off the Panzer's thick upper casemate section. Only a blackened, partial lower chassis and the tank's scorched road wheels and treads remained. Twisted portions of the steel casemate littered the area. The force of the blast toppled part of the stone wall onto the slit trench and the old Observation Post. A jeep-like *Kübelwagen* lay upside down beside the ruins of the Solvay's farmhouse, perhaps flipped by the massive detonation's force as well.

Other mines had blown around the wreckage during the attack or resulting explosion, but a few remained intact. Ruts in the farm field and the opposite road shoulder showed where later traffic had detoured in retreat, swerving around the destroyed vehicle. A burned-out half-track blocked the road farther north, another victim of Allied air power.

146

Cooper repositioned the few remaining mines to the detour spot in the field in case of further incursion. The men spliced cut field telephone wire and checked the lines north and south for German wires tapping in.

Burnanski helped Joe limp and stumble over to the old Observation Post, now a jumble of snow, dirt, chunks of wood and stones from the wall. The rest of the squad finished moving mines and splicing wire. They shuffled back up to clear the other foxholes for the approaching night. Joe kept watch while Burnanski labored on, clearing out snow, branches and stones. Joe could see Burnanski's face, gaunt with exhaustion and lack of food. Every clumsy motion eroded last reserves of energy. Finally Burnanski slumped down, sitting on the edge of the hole.

Only the lower section of one of the two large trees by the outpost remained upright, its bark scored away on the eastern side by the blast from the destroyed assault gun. Joe stood above the foxhole in the shadow of the trunk, supporting his injured leg by leaning against the trunk's war-beaten surface. He forced his tired eyes to focus as he peered out past the tank's wreckage, across the frozen woods and snow-covered fields. "Seems like we've been here for months."

Burnanski stared down at the ground for several minutes. When he finally spoke, in words thick and labored by weariness, "Some . . . some Christmas, huh?" He paused and swallowed. "Half . . . half frozen, half starved. Never had much as a kid, but even that was better than this." He looked up at Joe with haggard face and blood-shot eyes. "How 'bout you?"

Joe glanced toward him. "I'm sure worn out. But when I start focusing on how miserable I feel, I keep remembering how Jesus came on the first Christmas so that He might go on to the cross and suffer more than this."

"You think about Jesus a lot."

"He's the only thing that keeps me going."

Burnanski's thoughts seemed to be operating in slow motion. Perplexed, he asked, "Why . . . why'd He do it? Why'd He suffer and die like the Bible says?"

"Because He loves us."

"That's . . . awfully simple."

"Simple enough that a child can understand. A lot of folks stumble over that."

Emotional and physical strain bore down on Burnanski. He began shuddering from exhaustion as he said, "I'm . . . I'm so tired, so tired. Not just . . . this war, but of feeling . . . feeling so rotten inside."

"Jesus wants to take that from you," Joe replied. "He said, 'Come unto me, all ye that labor and are heavy laden and I will give you rest.' Jesus can give you new life free from the burden of sin and bring rest for your soul."

Burnanski's shuddering subsided. He rubbed his palms on his thighs and took a deep breath. He sat still for a moment, forcing himself to listen to the forest and trying to sort out what he'd seen and felt in the last few days. He thought about the answered prayer he'd witnessed and the words Joe had just said. Something remained beyond his understanding. He slowly shook his head. With a great effort he finally said, "I'm too . . . too tired to figure this out. I . . . I know now that God is real, but . . . but I'm still not sure about the . . . the *love* you say He has for me. What . . . what love can He have for a sinner like me?"

Joe kept his gaze on the field beyond the road, and answered, "The Bible says, '. . . God commendeth His love toward us, in that while we were yet sinners, Christ died for us.' *Commendeth* means 'to show, to prove.' God proved His love when Jesus died for you and me. If you could see Jesus right now, all you'd have to do is look at His nail-pierced hands to know how much He loves you. Sure, God hates sin, but He paid the penalty for it Himself so that He might save those who believe on Him. It will always remain beyond complete human understanding. That's part of where faith comes in, trusting God for all the rest."

Joe fumbled at the opening of his field jacket with fingers stiff from cold and awkward from fatigue. He reached inside, pulled out a small leather-bound book and offered it to Burnanski. "I've wanted you to have this Bible; then you can read about it for yourself. I've already marked some verses for you."

Burnanski shook his head. "I . . . I couldn't take your Bible from you."

Joe's injured leg had gone stiff. With an effort, he bent down and offered the Bible again. "The Lord laid it on my heart. I have a bigger one with our stuff back in France and one of those little pocket New Testaments to get me by for now. Think of this Bible as a Christmas present from me to you."

Awed by the personal gesture, Burnanski carefully took the small book from Joe and flipped through it. It appeared even smaller in his large hands. "Wow. Never . . . never had a Bible . . . of my own before." After turning a few times seeing places where Joe had underlined verses, he opened his jacket and slid the book into a jumpsuit pocket. He patted the small bulge it made. It felt good having it resting there.

Silent minutes crept by, weariness overshadowing each man like the real shadows lengthening on the countryside around them. Burnanski sat dazed on the edge of the foxhole while Anderson kept watch and silently prayed for him.

Behind them, the pale winter sun slowly sank behind the ridge, leaving the lower slope where they sat illumined only by the pale gibbous moon high overhead. The shattered forest left little cover now. The men clearing foxholes up near the crest moved as dark silhouettes against the pallid winter sunset.

Joe thought for a moment about his mom and sister. He closed his eyes a few seconds and could see their faces. He missed them. He felt the outside of his uniform for the inner pocket containing his wallet with their photograph in it and held it tight. He knew their thoughts and prayers were with him as well.

Everything across the darkening field appeared peaceful and still. Beyond that, only a few minutes of direct sunlight remained for the farm before the long shadow of the ridge enveloped the farmhouse ruins in twilight shadow.

A small flock of birds rose in sudden flight away from the farmhouse. Joe ran his tongue along his chapped lips, puzzling over why the birds would be flying so close to sunset when they ought to be settling in for the night. Something flashed in the distance. A brief, sharp flash. Joe forced himself erect, grabbing onto the rough bark of the tree and leaning against it for support. Something had stirred the birds up from their evening roost. Something had flashed, reflecting the remains of the late afternoon sun. *A mirror? A vehicle window? Someone's field-glasses?* "Ski, something's not right here." Joe lifted the O.P's captured field-glasses to his eyes and scanned across the farm, seeking the source of the flash. Down by the ruined house another brief flash. Joe saw the tops of helmets moving beyond the debris. "Germans! Dozens of them. Got to alert the Lieutenant!"

Burnanski had fallen asleep, slumped in a sitting position. Disoriented by Joe's sudden words, he muttered, "Huh?"

Joe dropped into the foxhole next to Burnanski. He fumbled with the field telephone in the darkness, cranked the generator, identified himself and said, "Sir, Germans moving around behind the Solvay farmhouse. Maybe a platoon."

The Lieutenant's terse voice came over the wire. "I'm taking a look east from up here." A moment later he said, "I see more. Another group pulling camouflage netting off a couple of half-tracks. 'Screaming Mimi's' mounted on them! Get out of there pronto! We're falling back. It's a trap!"

Burnanski had passed out again. Joe crawled out of the foxhole and shook him. "Ski! We're moving back on the double. Enemy fire's coming!"

Joe hobbled up the slope. He froze as a German flare burst high overhead and hung suspended beneath its parachute. Another and another, the flares' magnesium brilliance flooded the ridge-line with light.

Double streams of bullets zipped overhead as German machine guns opened fire from the east. Tracers crisscrossed along the illumined ridge-line, seeking Americans out in the open. Deep thumps from heavy mortars firing, the whirring of their shells arcing overhead mingled with the sickening "torn canvas" sound of in-coming 88mm artillery. The ground erupted in flame and thunder before and behind the company's positions overlooking the road.

Joe turned and saw groggy Burnanski, illuminated by the flash of explosions, still sitting out in the open. Joe scrambled back and shoved Burnanski into the foxhole, falling in on top of him.

The earth shook over and over again. Shells burst in the remaining trees. Deadly splinters rained down with the white-hot shrapnel. The Screaming Mimi's added the shrill howling of their rockets to the murderous onslaught.

Back up the ridge, the squad hunkered down in their holes, praying nothing would come their way. Showers of snow, frozen earth and parts of trees rained down on them. The shrieking rockets overshot the foxholes in that area, blasting the unoccupied ravine behind, but the 88mm artillery and heavy mortars pounded all along the ridge-line. The deafening explosions rolled on and on, tossing men about in their foxholes like rag dolls.

Slow in responding, American artillery returned fire. At the Lieutenant's direction, they pounded the rocket battery and drove German artillery observers, infantry and mortar crews away from the farm. The local barrage lessened because of that but continued in fury up the line around the northern roadblock. Survivors from the Lieutenant's platoon rose from their foxholes coughing and brushing away the debris. Several cried out for the medic. The barrage cut the telephone wires, so the Lieutenant sent

Reynolds running along, passing the word for squads to fall back near the aid station on the double and regroup against an attack.

Burnanski, coming awake through the quaking and thunder, found himself buried beneath falling earth and snow, chunks of wood and Joe Anderson's body. The whole terrible artillery storm shook him over and over. When the violent blasts subsided, he shouted for Joe to move so he could get up, but the rubble burying them muffled his cries. With an immense effort, he forced himself erect, lifting Joe up as well, out of the debris-filled hole.

Acrid smoke from the blasts filled the night air. The tree Joe had been leaning against before the barrage had taken a direct hit. Its pulverized stump smoldered, shattered pieces of the trunk now lay across the road. Splinters and branches littered the foxhole and the surrounding ground. Most of the remaining rock wall had collapsed into the slit trench. The barrage continued in the distance, threatening a return.

Burnanski tugged at the limp body of Joe Anderson. The horror of what had happened flooded over him. "Joe! Not you! NO! NO! NO!"

Burnanski shook the body again and again. No response. No pulse. He cried out in anguish, "Why God? Why'd it have to be Joe?!"

Shaking from grief, he gently laid the remains of Private Joe Anderson back into the foxhole. He tugged a torn blanket out of the wreckage and draped it over the body.

Hearing Burnanski's cries, Cooper and Wilcox came scrambling down over the forest wreckage to the road, fearing the worst. Distant flashes showed them Burnanski kneeling by the O.P. foxhole.

"You guys okay?" Wilcox called.

"We've gotta clear out of here on the double," yelled Cooper as he came.

Moonlight revealed the lifeless form in the foxhole. The pair fell to their knees beside Burnanski.

"Joe's gone," Burnanski said in a voice choked with emotion.

A void beyond expression enveloped the trio as they stared into that dim foxhole.

In the distance, Reynolds hollered down last call for everyone to withdraw on the double. The three struggled to their feet and gathered weapons. With increasing speed, they hurried from that cruel scene. Hot tears streamed down Wilcox's cheeks. Wetness also streaked Cooper's dirty face. Burnanski glanced back over his shoulder again and again into the darkness behind.

CHAPTER SIXTEEN

A New Position

December 25, 1944

The Squad

The entire battalion moved back, consolidating the perimeter, bracing for German night attack. For Burnanski, Wilcox, Cooper and the others, the dark hours passed in emotional and mental numbness. The cover of night hid their sorrow and insulated them from their physical weariness as they shuffled through snow and the bleak woods to their new position. They labored through the evening, piercing the frozen ground, digging themselves in.

The moon set. An attack never materialized in that sector. The only fighting came far off to the left around the north roadblock. Distant noises from unseen armored vehicles came from American forces. The "Bastogne Fire Brigade" headed off once more, blunting the newest thrust of the Panzers down a main road to the northeast. In the middle of the night, patrols returned. The squad stood down and tried getting some sleep, but sleep wouldn't come.

Cooper and Wilcox crawled over to Burnanski. They found him sitting alone in his dark foxhole, his head down, holding a small leather book.

"That's Joe's little Bible, isn't it?" Cooper said.

"He gave it to me," Burnanski said. "Minutes later, he died." He stood up in the hole and sat down on its edge. Cooper and Wilcox slumped down beside him.

Burnanski continued cradling the small book in his hands. They sat in silence for a long moment. When Burnanski finally spoke, agony and guilt filled his voice. "I gotta talk 'bout Joe. He saved my miserable life again. I musta passed out when the Krauts shelled us. He pushed me into that hole. I came out alive; but he didn't. When we first took up position in the woods by that road, I hated him and all he stood for. Told him that the foxhole he dug would be his grave. Now it's come true."

Cooper took out his toothpick, snapped it in half and flicked it away. "Not in the way you meant. Joe wouldn't want you to think that."

Wilcox remembered the conversation he had with Joe after Burnanski's prediction on that day. "Think of what Joe tried showing us about Christ—the greatest love—the love which sent Christ to give His life for all of us miserable sinners."

"You can't blame yourself," Cooper said. "That'd only continue the bitterness n' guilt that's been eatin' at you."

"Joe didn't see you or anyone as a problem," Wilcox said. "He saw us all as souls in a battle, souls needing Christ."

Burnanski held up the book, leafing through the pages at random. He dropped down in his foxhole and took out his lighter. For a horrible moment, the others thought he would burn the Bible. Instead, he held the flame carefully away from the open book and peered at its pages in the flickering light. "Look!" he said. "Joe marked some verses. What's this one?"

Wilcox dropped into the hole beside him, and Cooper squeezed in too. Wilcox took out his GI flashlight and flicked it on, silently thanking whoever had thought to send fresh batteries in the last airdrop. Shielding the narrow beam of light so it wouldn't attract either the Germans or a rebuke from Reynolds, he peered at the tiny type on the small page. "It's the Gospel of John," he said, "chapter one, verse twelve." He took the book and held it to his face, squinting to get a closer look. "It says, *But as many as received Him, to them gave He power to become the sons of God, even to them that believe on His name.*'"

Wilcox snapped off the light. They sat up on the edge of the foxhole again. All remained silent. The darkness made it hard to tell what the others thought.

Burnanski shifted his weight. "What should I do?" he asked.

"What should we all do?" added Cooper.

Wilcox thought, *If I'd ever read that verse or heard it in Sunday school as a kid, it had never made sense before. Now it's as plain as day.* He said, "We need to do what that verse tells us to do, what we know now Joe wanted over and over for us all to do. Each of us needs to pray and receive Christ as Savior."

"Help me," Burnanski said.

Three war-weary men bowed their heads together in prayer. They struggled with the words, but each poured his heart out before God who looks on the hearts of all men. They prayed by faith, without which it is impossible to please God, turning from sin and trusting in His Son for salvation. The battle for Bastogne was not yet over, but the battle more desperate, Joe Anderson's battle for their eternal souls, had been won.

* * * * * * *

On December 26th, a combat command from the 4th Armored Division, led by Lt. Col. Creighton Abrams, burst through the German lines. The siege of Bastogne ended. The Battle of the Bulge raged on for five more wintry weeks of heavy fighting. The airborne divisions joined the counterattack, cutting off Germans in the Bulge. The Wehrmacht paid dearly for Hitler's gamble, losing over 100,000 casualties, hundreds of irreplaceable tanks and trucks, and other essential equipment. Instead of quickly ending the war in the West, Hitler hastened his personal doom five months later.

* * * * * * *

GREIER

The jaded column wound its way back east. Only a small fraction remained from the superb Panzer unit that slashed through American lines three weeks before. Their angry wave crashed upon a granite shore and spent its strength against the stalwart defense of Bastogne. Instead of flowing through weakened defenses, slaughtering their foes and advancing to victory, American tanks and reinforced infantry flooded out upon them, turning the tide of battle.

SS troops and Volksgrenadier stragglers now trudged along back toward the Vaterland's border. Greier had driven them eastward all night long. Dawn approached. His exhausted men wondered if he'd halt them soon.

The SS-Sturmbannführer rode ahead of his men. His arm still hung in a sling, a smaller bandage on his head. He stood in the open hatch of his Panther command tank, mulling over the bitter situation. *How could this happen to us? To me? We gripped an egg in our mailed fist, ready to crush its thin shell, only to have it hatch a viper and be stung by its fangs!*

He grimaced, seeing the tattered remnants of his once powerful Sturmbataillion. The Amerikaner counterattack disintegrated flanking units, exposing Greier's tanks and men. Bazookas and captured Panzerfaust picked off SturG's one by one. The last two tanks drained of fuel for his Panther and abandoned.

Doubt rippled through Greier again. He pushed the nagging uncertainty aside with thoughts of recrimination, *Worthless Volksgrenadier— old women and little girls! Surrendering to the Americans rather than standing with us to fight! I'll never surrender while the Führer lives! His curse upon those cowards! And upon the smug Amerikaner! Upon the Adlerkopf Fallschirmjäger! The terror you would've felt in defeat will be magnified a hundred-fold the next time we meet in battle! I'm not through yet!*

The frantic calling of Greier's worried little adjutant jogged him from his reverie. *Mousy little man!* Greier scoffed to himself. *Trotting along like a schoolgirl hailing a trolley conductor!*

"Mein Herr! Mein Herr! The fog is lifting!" the man shouted. "We must leave the road now and shelter beneath the trees. Jabos will prey upon us if we continue in the open!"

Greier turned, scanning the sky. The sun had risen above the eastern ridges. The foggy curtain dissipated. The thinning veil revealed a heartening sight—rows upon rows of concrete *Drachenzähne* tank obstacles glowed in the brilliant dawn, zigzagging along the near slopes less than a kilometer away. *The Siegfried Line! Soon we'll pass through the frontier defenses back upon the Vaterland's sacred soil.* Something more—many black dots moving in the blue high above, approaching from the east! *The Luftwaffe at last! Air cover the rest of the way home!*

"Stop fussing like an old *Schwiegermutter*!" Greier jeered down at the adjutant. He pointed to the sky. "Can't you see the Vaterland is just ahead? Even now our Führer sends his mighty angels of protection!"

A different kind of angels high overhead banked around, shifting into single file attack formation, swooping down upon his column.

* * * * * * *

SQUADRON LEADER

Patience, lads, thought the squadron leader. *Good things come to those who wait!*

His flight of six RAF Typhoon fighter-bombers took off from muddy advance airfields south of Namur before dawn, hunting over German territory behind the West Wall at first light. Heavy fog covered barge and rail traffic in the Mosel River Valley, their intended targets. They orbited above, but the heavy river fog showed no sign of lifting. His aircraft headed back west now with nothing to show for their early morning effort.

The leader's Hawker Typhoon, "Tiffy 'Tilda," was the only aircraft in his flight carrying eight RP-3 rockets. Their sixty-pound warheads combined in a force greater than the salvo from a navy cruiser's guns. Other planes carried two 500 pound bombs a piece. *Shame to return to base with this ordinance*, the Squadron Leader thought. *Dicey trying to land with it still under the wings.*

Dark shapes crawled along a forest road far below, like a stream of ants—a retreating German column emerged from shreds of thinning ground fog into the bright sun light. Mostly on foot. Some vehicles. Some horse-drawn artillery. *Targets of opportunity at last!*

The leader radioed his charges, "Red Leader to Red Flight. Jerry column heading east along the forest road at 9:00. Jettison drop tanks. Red Two, lead the way. I'll clean up." He dropped his extra fuel tank and pulled away from the other aircraft, ready to follow in their wake.

Red Number Two brought his Typhoon, "Barmy Beast," into optimal position on the column. The rest of the flight trailed behind him, mirroring his tight, banking turn back around to the east. The maneuver brought the bright sun to their backs, into the eyes of their foes below. Red Two dived down on the roadway, initiating the attack. Beads on a string, following aircraft spread out and descended behind him one by one. Picking up speed. The increasing howl of their rapid swoop declared a violent intent.

"Tally-ho!" Red Two shouted as he roared along the retreating column with blazing 20mm cannon. He lifted his wings right, then left, dropping each bomb onto the widening chaos below. Four trailing aircraft swept either side of the road with equal effect.

Men on the ground fell on the roadway. Survivors scrambled for cover. Horses reared in panic. Vehicles caught fire, swerved off the road. Munitions exploded.

"There's one for you, Red Leader. Tank at the head of the column."

"Thank you, Red Two. I'm on the blighter now."

The Squadron Leader adjusted his aircraft, swinging into line on the lumbering target, one worthy of his rockets at last. With a deadly precision born of experience, he launched his full rocket salvo at the vulnerable rear of a large tank now crawling alone out on the road, ahead of the smoking carnage. *Thanks, old boy, for taking them off my hands!*

* * * * * * *

GROSSHOLTZ

"For you the war is over!" Oberfeldwebel Grossholtz muttered the time-worn phrase spoken to the many Amerikaner prisoners of the war just a few weeks before. Now he applied it to himself as well. *Yes, over for me at long last. Time now to clean up and rebuild from the terrible waste it had wrought,* he thought. An *Evangelischer-Christian,* he'd often regretted his loyalty oath to the nation's supreme leader. He felt released now from the entanglement of those empty words. *My supreme loyalty in the future will only be toward Jesus Christ.*

Grossholtz's unit had surrendered, one of those shattered and surrounded in the Bulge. His wounds did not prevent him from assisting his captors in identifying and recovering the dead bodies, both Amerikaner and Deutsch, from the recent battlefield. He had personally led them through the woods to places where he knew his own young and old men had fallen, especially in the remains of their Biwak, scorched by Allied fighter-bombers.

This morning, he stood beside a truck supervising a P.O.W. detail of his own men as they lifted up the remains of yet another dead Amerikaner Fallschirmjäger. He remembered this particular area well. His unit suffered through a bitter fight in the woods to the north. Near-by on patrol, he had heard the Adlerköpfe singing. Later, he and his men, supported by the SS-Sturmbataillion, assaulted this ridge-line, only to find the *Schützenlöchern* empty. Later, they lured the Amerikaner back and caught them a fierce artillery barrage. One of them had died here in a hole beyond the ruins of a stone wall. The work detail lifted the remains, a frozen body draped by a torn blanket.

Such waste! thought Grossholtz. *So many, so young, like this one. So full of promise, cut short by war. It darkens my soul.*

The P.O.W. detail carried the stiff body onto the truck and laid it beside the others. The armed guards and Grossholtz himself ensured all proceeded with care. Before spreading the torn blanket back over the body, one dog tag was removed. A guard read the name and rank and service number and jotted them on his clipboard. He noted the location coordinates as well. He added the tag to a growing collection, for further processing later.

Something had fallen from the body onto the snow. The shuffling feet of the detail kicked the small object beneath the truck. Grossholtz crouched down, picked it up and brushed off the snow. *A little book.* He flipped its pages. *A Tasche Neue Testament in English! This young man was a Christian, perhaps a fellow believer! That's a bit of light shining in the darkness of all this death. Perhaps here's one who brought some solace to his comrades and a measure of hope into a war-troubled world before he died. A least it does to me now, to think of him this way. God in Heaven, thank you for that!*

Grossholtz handed the pocket New Testament over to the guard collecting the dog tags. The guard noted it on his clipboard and dropped it into a box with other soldiers' miscellaneous personal effects. The truck started up. It crept on along to the next of many stops that day. Grossholtz and the other P.O.W.'s tramped along the snowy road in its wake.

* * * * * * *

THE ANDERSONS

A week after the relief of Bastogne, a telegram arrived at the Anderson home in Illinois. A terse message typed on yellow paper, sent from the War Department, signed by the adjutant general. An officer from Fort Sheridan rode the Chicago and Northwestern commuter line west to the village of Glen Ellyn. The Anderson's pastor, contacted beforehand, met the officer at the station. They drove together up to the Anderson's home. The officer hand-delivered the telegram in the living room.

The message read in part: *"The Secretary of War desires me to express his deepest regrets to inform you that Joseph W. Anderson, Private, U.S. Army was killed in action defending his country on Twenty-five December in Belgium. Pvt. Anderson has been awarded the Purple Heart posthumously for wounds received on Twenty-three December."*

That evening a banner with a gold star hung in the front window.

Two weeks later Joe Anderson's final letter, written on V-mail from a makeshift basement aid station in Bastogne days before he died, reached his home:

Dear Mom and Susan,

These Christmas greetings will be a little late getting to you. Our mail service has been temporarily interrupted.

I write this from a basement aid station. I've been wounded, but I'll be O.K. Your prayers, no doubt, kept me safe from more serious wounds. Just needed some stitches along my upper right leg. I hurt it worse that time I ran my sled into the hay rake on Uncle Mel's farm when I was nine.

I send you all my love. Part of me wishes to be with you, and yet I have a tremendous desire to be here and serve the Lord. In that desire I have great peace.

I need to get back to my squad. I know they need me, not just because of my weapon, but because they need the Gospel.

You've probably heard of our situation. The enemy has us been hitting us hard, but there's also a spiritual battle going on. Satan has the hearts of men under siege, but the Gospel can defeat him. If something should ever happen to me, it'll be worth it all, not only if it brought us closer to an Allied victory over the Nazis, but also if it brought the men I serve with to know the greatest love of all, the love of Jesus Christ.

Love,

Joe

Philippians 1:21 "For me to live is Christ; to die is gain."

In early February, after the fighting in Belgium died down, one more letter arrived at the Anderson's home:

Dear Mrs. Anderson,

I'm not very good at this, but I wanted to write you. By now, you know that Joe died in the fighting at Bastogne. I was with him then.

I once hated Joe and picked on him because I was mad at God, but God didn't give up on me, and Joe didn't either. I want you to know that Joe didn't die in vain. He died saving my life, just after showing me that Jesus loved me and gave Himself for me. I received Christ as my Savior later that night, and so did two other men Joe had been witnessing to. The next day, three more trusted the Lord, and I heard another had received Christ while Joe was at an aid station in town. That makes up our whole squad, going into the battle. What a great victory for Joe's Savior and for Joe himself!

I also want you to know that I have Joe's small Bible. He gave it to me as a Christmas present just before he died. I will treasure it always.

I'm only a new Christian, but by God's grace, I'm trying to tell every G.I. I can about the love of Christ, and demonstrate it, just like Joe did. The Lord has really changed my life. Because of that, some other guys in our platoon are now also trusting in Christ.

I know Joe was studying to be a preacher, and now I believe God is leading me to take his place. When this war is over, somehow, with God's help, I'm going to study for that ministry too. Like Joe, I'm ready to give my life telling others about the greatest love!

In Christ,

Sergeant Wendell Burnanski

II Corinthians 9:15, "Thanks be unto God for His unspeakable gift!"

EPILOGUE

Harrisburg, Pennsylvania

December 2004

Wilcox

You wake as the notebook falls to the floor. You fell asleep while reading it again.

The morning nurse comes in to check on you with her usual quiet efficiency. She picks up the tattered notebook and places it again in your hands. "Here's your journal, Mr. Wilcox. How are you feeling today?"

Low humidity of the healthcare facility's filtered air makes your throat dry. "'Bout the same," you rasp out in a thin whisper. It's true, and yet you know it will be soon. Hopefully, your dear wife will return before then. She'd headed home late last night to get a few hours of needed rest.

You're offered breakfast. You eat little. *Don't need much to keep going now,* you think to himself. *Just the company of my wife, or reading from my Bible or the pages of my journal.*

Following what has become your daily routine, you're helped from the bed into a wheelchair still holding onto your tattered old journal. Doors open, and you're wheeled over into the common room for the rest of the morning. The room is warm. Sunlight streams in through the large windows. Several bright red poinsettias and a Christmas tree with twinkling lights have taken up residence in a corner opposite the door, and some romantic has even hung a sprig of mistletoe above the doorway, preparations for a Christmas you know you probably won't see.

Cancer has silently spread through your body. Undetected until too late.

"Inoperable," doctors said. "Try to make his last days as comfortable as possible." And they had. Your wife is constantly at your side. Children, grandchildren, and even great-grandchildren come to cheer you. Your young pastor visits or calls almost every day. Church members drop in. Former students and colleagues come to see you or call, send cards, flowers and e-mail.

A few weeks more, a few days more, perhaps a few hours more, you think. *A short time to reflect on life and death. I've faced death before, more violent and abrupt than the gradual something I'm facing now. The grace of God is sufficient for both.*

You open the cracked leather cover of your little journal and look at its stained, worn pages. Some are so smudged they're barely illegible, but you know what is recorded there by heart. *Like me*, you think, *years before, this journal had been fresh and new. Now, like me, it's faded and frayed, soon to be laid to rest somewhere.*

You are ready to depart, been ready for a long, long time. Only that God has some remaining purpose yet for you has prolonged your earthly sojourn.

They're waiting for me over there, on the other side. Joe Anderson, Cooper, the Lieutenant and others have gone on before. Soon I'll see them again, those I've greatly loved and missed. And soon I'll see Him face to face, the One who's shown me the Greatest Love of All.

You pause, gazing out of the window down at snow covered lawns and the freshly plowed parking lot. No one else around, the first in after breakfast, you pick up the remote control and click off the loud chatter of the morning show hosts. You chuckle with muted glee at cutting off the incessant noise.

That's better. Prefer doing my own thinking. Only a little while, a little while is left. Grateful, Lord Jesus, for this remaining time to think about the near future or treasure the past. I'll turn these pages once more, read their names and remember them with You, Lord, that special squad You gave me sixty years ago at Bastogne.

Joe Anderson—Thank you, Lord, for how he lived and how he died. He wanted to serve You as well as his country, and he did—Oh, how he did!

Cooper—Thank you, Lord, for him too, killed in January '45, attacking the machine gun that pinned us down during our counterattack through a Belgian village. Bronze Star. Miss him every day.

Thank you for the Lieutenant. Was wounded, but survived the war. Burnanski led him to you while on occupation duty in Bavaria. Stayed in the army. Commanded a battalion in Korea, assistant commander of an Air Cavalry Brigade in

Vietnam—always shepherding the next bunch of youngsters! Retired with one star and became an adjunct professor at his Alma Mater. Head usher at his church. Now he's gone to be with You.

Thank you for Reynolds. Struggled with alcohol after the war, a failed marriage. Burnanski went to see him and led him to You! He ran a construction business in Little Rock after that and taught Sunday school. Retired to Arizona. Gone to be with You, as well.

Thank You for Friedenfeld. Returned to cattle ranching in Wyoming, married a pastor's daughter, was a deacon in his church and served on the county board. In a nursing home now in Laramie. Doesn't remember anyone anymore, but You haven't forgotten him, and neither have I!

Thank You for Vincenti. He returned to his old Philly neighborhood and worked his way up to supervisor in the city's sanitation department, was a faithful church member and on the board of trustees for a Rescue Mission. Came to see me with his wife last month. He has cancer too.

Thank You for Nurnberg. He joined his dad and uncle working at the motorcycle plant, eventually becoming a shop steward. Active in the local Christian community, helped start a Christian radio station. Retired now, a part-time maintenance man at a Wisconsin youth camp. Exchanged Christmas cards, the last I'll send.

Thank you for Tobin. After rehab, he enrolled in college on the G.I. Bill, became a teacher himself and a high school baseball coach in Central California. Volunteered weekends at a ministry for disabled veterans. Automobile accident took him home to be with You over thirty years ago.

Thank you for what you've done in my own life. Wounded the day before we withdrew from Belgium. Time in the hospital gave me ample time to study the Bible and really understand it for the first time. Through rehab and mustered out in September '45. Back in the classroom by the second semester.

Harriet had finished college during the war and came on the faculty the fall of '45. She'd written me, and I'd written her, when I was overseas. I'd exchanged letters with other former students too, but she'd had a crush since her student days, dreamed of marrying me if I came back from the war unattached. Who'd have thought of one of the prettiest girls had set her cap for the scruffy "Mr. Chips" of Raphoe Academy! Thank you, for her too.

Some of the squad came for our wedding, the first of our reunions scattered through the years. The school closed after a post-war financial decline. Harriet and I moved here, taught in the community college, worked on our master's degrees, raised our son and daughters. I earned my doctorate and became head of the history department. Wrote a couple books on the Civil War, some articles for popular history magazines.

Both of us sang in the church choir, worked in children's Bible clubs. I chaired the missions committee. Thanks for the opportunity to serve You together!

Then there's Burnanski—Thank You for the miracle of a transformed life in all of us, none more dramatically transformed than in Burnanski! He became a top soldier again and so much more. Replaced me as squad leader and became platoon sergeant again after Reynolds was wounded a month later. Continued in the service for two more years, training the new troopers while he caught up on education he'd missed.

Went off to study for the ministry at the same school Joe Anderson had attended. A girl from the student council met new students at the train station when he arrived, brought them out to the campus and helped them register. She was Joe's kid sister, Susan! Susan became like a sister to Burnanski as well. Through Susan, You led Burnanski to Francine, her best friend on campus, a former WAC from Georgia.

Wendell and Francine have been married over fifty years now, three children, five grandchildren—all in some ministry for You, or preparing for one. Served almost twenty years themselves as missionaries in East Africa before continuing bouts of malaria threatened their health. Another seventeen years ministering to servicemen and their families stationed in Germany. Still going strong in semi-retirement, on the staff of a church outside an army base in Kentucky now, counseling more young soldiers. Leading more souls to You!

Talked to him on the phone last week. He'll speak at my memorial service. Thank You for that too, and work in many hearts through his words! Told him to preach Your gospel, just like we heard it from Joe, taking his text from John 15:13 and building his message around the story of our time together in the woods outside Bastogne.

Later that afternoon, your condition worsens. You wake up the next day with an I.V. tube poking into your arm and wires running to sensors taped to your chest. Harriet is beside you, has been all night, holding your hand. Tears well up in her eyes as you turn your head and give her a weak smile.

"I love you," you manage to whisper. *Such an effort now to speak.*

"And I love you,' she says and kisses you. She holds you close for a long time.

"God is good. He's waiting for me," you struggle to say. "Anderson . . . and . . . and Cooper and the others . . . also . . . waiting. And I . . . I'll be waiting . . . for you, darling."

She embraces you again, sobbing softly.

With a great effort, you lift your hand to her hair, a final caress. Hand drops. Eyes close. Absent from the body, you enter the presence of your Lord. Home at last, beyond sin and sorrow, pain and weakness. Flooded with light and peace and incredible joy.

Back in the room, your journal falls to the floor again. Monitors sound an alarm. Nurses and doctors rush in. They do what they can and depart a while later. Silence fills the room. A long time sitting beside your bed, your wife picks up your journal, closes it. She lifts your cold right hand and places it over the worn little notebook, resting them both above your no longer beating heart.

The End

Dear Reader

Although the characters and situations in this novel are fiction, men like Joe Anderson and Wendell Burnanski did exist. Back when I attended the school, plaques hanging at the War Memorial Chapel at Bob Jones University in Greenville, South Carolina remind us of their sacrifice and service. Those real soldiers--students and faculty from the college serving their Savior as they served their country--provided inspiration in creating Joe Anderson in the story. After the war, the Preacher's Classes at schools like BJU swelled with the ranks of men returning from the war and preparing for full-time Christian service—a model for what Burnanski in this story did with his life after salvation and wartime service.

What About You?

Have you put your personal trust in Christ alone for salvation? Has there been a time in your life when you prayed and asked Him to save your soul, like the members of the squad at the end of the story? That is the most desperate battle in your life and one you can win today through faith in the death, burial and resurrection of Jesus Christ. He loved you with that "greatest love" of John 15:13, laying down His life for you on the cross and now beckons for you to come to Him. If you haven't already, please call upon the Lord today and gain the eternal victory for that battle in your own life.

". . . Believe on the Lord Jesus Christ and thou shalt be saved."

Acts 16:31

You may contact the author by e-mail at *pilz.author@gmail.com*

Selected Background Material

Below is a partial list of background material for further study of the historical context and the Battle of the Bulge:

Band of Brothers: E Company, 2nd Battalion, 506th Parachute Infantry Regiment, 101st Airborne Division by Stephen Ambrose. One of the inspirations for the novel *A Battle More Desperate,* which began development around the question "What if a sold-out, soul-winning Christian arrived in the "Band of Brothers" just before the siege of Bastogne?"

Citizen Soldiers also by Stephen Ambrose, one of the most accurate and honest attempts to describe what it was like to be a common GI fighting in Northwest Europe in 1944-45.

Seven Roads to Hell by Donald Burgett. An excellent first-hand account of the siege of Bastogne from a member of the 101st Airborne who was there. Burgett's other personal reminiscences as a "Screaming Eagle," which include his experiences recorded in his books *Currahee!* (D-Day); *The Road to Arnhem* (Operation Market Garden) and *Beyond the Rhine: A Screaming Eagle in Germany* (Victory in Europe and beyond).

The Battle of the Bulge by William K. Goolrich, Ogden Tanner and the Editors of Time-Life Books. A volume in their W.W. II series. A good basic history of the battle with ample pictures.

The Homefront: U.S.A by Ronald H. Bailey and the Editors of Time-Life Books, another volume in the Timer-Life W.W. II series. An account of wartime events and civilian life inside the United States from before Pearl Harbor to V-E Day, V-J Day and beyond.

A Time for Trumpets: The Untold Story of the Battle of the Bulge by Charles MacDonald. Another anecdotal treatment with some information found nowhere else.

Battle: The Story of the Bulge by John Toland. An exhaustive classic of narrative and anecdotal perspectives.

Battleground, a classic movie depiction of the Battle of the Bulge produced only four years after the war. It is the fictional account (which glosses over some of the suffering) of a glider infantry squad in the 101st during the Siege of Bastogne. The screenwriter based the script, in part, on his own experiences during the battle, although he wasn't with the Airborne. The film won the 1950 Academy Awards for Best Cinematography, Black and White and Best Writing, Story and Screenplay. Actors include Van Johnson, James Whitmore, Ricardo Montelban, and George Murphy. Some actual 101st veterans filled supporting roles and acted as advisers.

Other Background Sources Worth Reading:

Ridgeway's Paratroopers by Clay Blair. A thorough history of U.S. Airborne troops from pre-war experimental units and organization of the first Parachute Infantry Regiments to combat in Europe through to the Allied occupation of Germany.

The Bitter Woods by John S. D. Eisenhower (Ike's son). Another anecdotal history of the battle with emphasis on the allied commands from the Supreme Commander down to squad leaders.

Patton: Ordeal and Triumph by Lasadas Farrago, A detailed account of Gen. George Patton in World War II. One of the primary sources for the movie *Patton*.

The Damned Engineers by Janice Holt Giles. The fascinating record of how a small, resourceful unit of American combat engineers frustrated and stalled part of the northern German advance in the Battle of the Bulge, written by the wife of one of the engineers.

I was Baker Two by J.J. Kuhn. A unique personal account by a West Bend, Wis. native of his W.W. II experience which included being taken prisoner at the beginning of the Battle of the Bulge and his experiences as a prisoner of war afterward.

ABOUT THE AUTHOR

Randy Pilz is the father of five wonderful children and proud grandfather of three precious grandchildren.

Born and raised in Chicagoland, Randy trusted in Jesus Christ as his Savior through a community Bible study during his junior year in high school (the character Joe Anderson's testimony in this novel is partly based on Randy's real testimony). After salvation, the Lord led him to Bob Jones University, where he studied Bible, Speech and Drama.

Called to Christian service, Randy served "two tours of duty" as a Christian school teacher. He later became drama director at Falls Baptist Church in Menomonee Falls, Wis. Through that ministry he began writing plays and programs as tools for local church evangelism.

For eleven years, Randy served as a Creative Director/Video Producer on the staff at Pensacola Christian College, producing promotional and educational videos and assisting in the production of the *Rejoice in the Lord* telecast. He later worked as an independent producer in a non-profit media ministry.

A Battle More Desperate is Randy's first published novel. His next prospective works include a novel about the Biblical character Simon of Cyrene; a short historical novel set in 1811 based the Old Testament book of Jonah; and a re-telling of *A Christmas Carol*.

www.ingramcontent.com/pod-product-compliance
Lightning Source LLC
Chambersburg PA
CBHW060423130626
46555CB00005B/2196